PRAISE FOR HELEN DUNMORE'S

Talking to the Dead

"Dunmore takes a tale that could drive a thriller and weaves her linguistic spell around it. The result is brilliant and terrifying, an unbeatable combination. . . . We aren't released from the author's spell until the novel's very last line."
— Carolyn Banks, *Washington Post*

"Sensual, delectable, and chilling. . . . Helen Dunmore's prose is limpid — the descriptions of food are voluptuous, the sex scenes urgent and raw — and her plotting is masterful."
— Paula Chin, *People*

"A gripping and lyrical study of past tragedy returning to haunt the present."   — Pat Barker, *Sunday Times* (London)

"A finely crafted short novel, both erotic and disturbing."
— Janet Cooper, *Providence Journal-Bulletin*

"A passionate, mysterious, and ultimately stunning work. . . . The reader discovers how damnably close the sisters were as the story wends its way through the British countryside in sensuous and mesmerizing fashion."
— Alice Evans, *Portland Oregonian*

"A profound novel. . . . Dunmore writes persuasively and with ardor that lures one into her world of secrets, pain, love, and ultimately death."
— Quinn Fitzpatrick, *Rocky Mountain News*

"Voluptuously written. . . . A tale of mayhem and seduction among the raspberry brambles. . . . Dunmore's understanding of the ways of guilt, loss, and transcendence make this a book of profound insight."
— Joe Cadora, *San Francisco Chronicle*

"Intense, fast-paced fiction. . . . You may stay up late to finish this one — it's that absorbing."   — *Mademoiselle*

ALSO BY HELEN DUNMORE

Your Blue-Eyed Boy

Talking to the Dead

A Novel

HELEN DUNMORE

LITTLE, BROWN AND COMPANY

Boston New York Toronto London

First U.S. edition published by Little, Brown and Company, 1997
First Back Bay paperback edition, 1998

The characters and events in this book are fictitious. Any similarity to real persons, living or dead, is coincidental and not intended by the author.

Excerpt from "Autobiography" from *Collected Poems* by Louis MacNeice. First published by Faber and Faber Ltd. Reprinted by permission of David Hingham Associates.

Library of Congress Cataloging-in-Publication Data
Dunmore, Helen
      Talking to the dead : a novel / Helen Dunmore. — 1st ed.
          p.   cm.
      ISBN 0-316-19741-6 (hc)   0-316-19645-2 (pb)
      I. Title
    PR6054.U528T35   1997
    823´. 914 — dc20   96-38726

10   9   8   7   6   5   4   3

Q-MART

Book design by Julia Sedykh

Printed in the United States of America

Talking to the Dead

prologue

THE NEWER GRAVES *lie full in the sun, beyond the shadow of the church and yew tree. Two of them are covered in plastic-wrapped flowers and raw earth; these graves won't have stones for a while yet, because they must wait for the earth to settle.*

There are a lot of things you need to learn when someone dies, and you have to learn fast, from people who are paid to teach you. They come up with hushed, serious faces and ask questions. If you don't say anything right away, they just wait. It's their job. There were two of them standing there, noting down the requirements. One glanced at the other, and they gleamed with satisfaction at phrasing it all so well. But they were much too professional to smile.

And then the food. After a funeral you have to eat, to prove you're still alive. There are foods that are suitable, and foods that are not. The suitable ones turn out to be ham, or cold chicken. Quiche is very popular, and Australian wines. I can remember staring at a big glazed ham, its rind scored into squares and glistening with syrup. I thought of how it would be sliced and fed to us after your burial. Someone was asking me if I would like fresh pineapple to garnish the ham, or tinned.

"Will you want the coffin open, or closed?"

"Some people," one of them whispered, "some people find it a great comfort actually to have seen. *Not to have to* imagine. *It can be a great comfort."*

"A great comfort," I say aloud now, taking the words out like stones from my pocket, tossing them into the quiet air.

It's beautiful here, where you are. Tall brick-and-flint walls enclose the churchyard, but we're high up, and the air moves freely. It's hot and dry, and the earth smells like a body stretched out to bake in the sun. Bees have swarmed on the other side of the church. I went round just now, and saw them hanging there in a dark cluster under the roof. Stray bees zinged through the air toward the swarm, and their sound was dangerous, like water in a kettle that has nearly boiled dry. I came away lightly, scarcely breathing.

You are out in the sun, away from the yew tree. Your stone stands firm. I know without looking exactly how many letters there are in the inscription. There is just your full name, the name you've kept since childhood, even after you married, and under your name, the dates of your birth and your death. No message, no reflection on your life. No clues at all. The only thing that might make anyone stop is the shortness of the time between the first date and the last. Someone might count up how long you'd lived, and wonder, and start to make up a story for you out of nothing.

People idling through graveyards always stop by the graves of the young. Hundreds of miles from here is another grave with the same surname on it as yours, a tiny grave in a steep cemetery above the sea. There's a path through the cemetery that tourists use as a shortcut down to the beach. They stop, read the inscription, the name and dates and the two lines of poetry. Often there's a jam jar of flowers left on the grave. If the tourists have children with them, they'll grasp their hands tightly as they walk on. I haven't been there for years. Did you go? Did you leave flowers there, and then stand looking down for a long time, thinking thoughts it's too late to uncover now?

I can almost see you. If I turn my head to the black splash of shade under the yew, now, quickly, I'm certain I'll see you. It's noon, the white hour when ghosts walk, leaving no shadow. But I don't turn my head. I still can't believe that you are here, near enough to touch if you weren't covered. I can't believe that if I dug down I would find first the quilting of earth, then the box, then you, yourself.

I lie down. I shut my eyes. I am in bed with you, warm

with the warmth of night. I feel your long slender legs curled up behind me, your knees digging into my back.

"Go to sleep."

"I am asleep."

"How can you be asleep when you're talking to me?"

And then silence. We are both asleep, tipping into the valley of the big double bed. None of this has happened yet.

I am on your grave, the warm mound of it shaped to me like a body. But though I listen and listen, there's no heartbeat. Your silence begins to soothe me. The air is warm. If I lie here long enough I'll begin to feel the earth turning beneath me, carrying everything away so that it can bring it back. Nothing can separate us.

I take a breath, and it comes out in your name. Isabel. You always answered. When I had a nightmare I would scream out your name. You'd kneel up beside me in your nightdress. "It's all right, Neen. I'm here."

"Isabel," I would say, "I had a bad dream . . ."

The soft breeze flutters in the grass. All the questions I am desperate to ask you float off, as the world floats off just before sleep.

chapter *one*

I SHOULD HAVE let the taxi take me all the way up to the house. I've packed more than usual, because I don't know how long I'll be staying, and the weather might change. I've brought some work stuff too — sketch pads, pencils, charcoal, inks. But only one camera. It feels strange to travel without my camera bag, the one I don't dare let out of my sight for a second. In London, at home, I haul it between the sweaty filth of the Underground and the heat of flats, shops, and offices. For weeks now it's been the hottest summer I can remember.

I like the early mornings and the smell when the pavement is being hosed down outside cafés. I drink coffee at six and I'm out by seven, when the sun's fresh on my arms, water drips from petunias in lamppost baskets, and vans whiz about full of new bread and newspapers with the print still damp on them. Then I know why I live in London. I'm on my way to meet someone for breakfast and what might just be a new, exciting piece of work. But by eleven the city's used up and

sweaty, and the new project's turned out to be photographing someone's day care scheme for a community
newspaper. I'm pushing at invisible barriers all the
time, never quite getting the work I really want. What
is it my pictures don't do?

No need to think about that now. I shift my bag to
the other hand and keep on up the rough track. It's getting dark, and all the white things look whiter still: the
tall stiff flowers in the hedge, the moths, and my skirt.
The air smells unnaturally sweet. There are owls here,
but I haven't seen one. Isabel knows about them. *A pair
of barn owls is nesting this year.*

In a way it's lucky I've got so much to carry, or I'd be
running, and then I'd arrive just the way I don't want to
arrive, hot and out of breath and anxious. And then
Richard would be angry. *Isabel can't cope with other people's emotions just now,* he said. She's not supposed to
know he told me to come. She won't like it; she'll say it's
interrupting my life and making me lose commissions,
when I've worked so hard to build things up. As if I
would want to be anywhere else but with her.

I was in the bath when the phone rang. I heard his
voice cutting through my recorded message: "Nina, if
you're there, pick up the phone. It's Richard, it's important." He knew I often left the answering machine on
while I was working. I jumped out of the bath and

grabbed the phone and a towel, and covered myself even though he couldn't see me.

"What's the matter? Is Izzy all right?"

"For God's sake, Nina, calm down."

"Has she had the baby?"

"Yes, she's had the baby."

"How is she, what is it, I mean —"

"A boy. It's a boy."

"A boy."

I clutched the phone, and drips of water ran down it. Isabel has a son. Even as I said the words to myself she grew older, more distant, passing through a door that swung shut in my face.

"Yes. But I'm afraid it didn't go quite as we hoped." I heard the tension in his voice now, in its curious flatness. I had imagined how I'd get this news so many times. Always it was Isabel phoning me, Isabel with the baby curled in her arm, both of them weary, but triumphant that they'd found each other at last.

I was glad it was a boy, not a girl. I hadn't let myself know before now how much I didn't want Isabel to have a daughter.

"What's happened?"

"I can't go into it all now. I'm at the hospital and they're going to let me see her soon."

"Richard, why's she in hospital? She was going to

have it at home." I heard my own voice, stupidly accusing.

"Well, she didn't. Her uterus ruptured. They just got the baby out in time," he snapped, as if it were my fault. I was silent, trying to work out what these words meant. *Uterus. Ruptured.*

"You mean she had a cesarean?"

"I mean she had a hysterectomy."

"Jesus."

We were silent. I thought of the wooden handmade rocking cradle, a stupid extravagance for one child.

"It was all going fine," he said, "just as she thought it would. She wasn't even lying down. The midwife was there, having a cup of tea with us while Isabel put some baby clothes to air. She couldn't keep still, she kept moving round." He paused. "That track," he said. "I'll make Wilkinson mend that effing track if it's the last thing I do."

Wilkinson is the farmer who owns their house. "Couldn't the ambulance get up it?" I asked.

"There wasn't time to wait for an ambulance. I drove and the midwife went in the back of the car with her."

"But she's all right," I stated. It wasn't bathwater on the phone now, it was sweat from my hand.

"She'll be all right," said Richard. He threw the monosyllables at me as if they were balls he was bowling too fast. But cricket isn't Richard's game. Richard is three-quarters Irish by blood. Maybe you'd guess it from his eyes, which are bluer than English eyes, and they go with dark hair and skin rather than English fairness. Or you'd guess it from a concentration in his features, which makes them look as if they've been pushed together. He's a big man, over six feet tall and bulky too. He makes me jump when I come on him suddenly in the house.

I didn't know the right questions to ask. I don't know anything about childbirth, or babies. I listened to the telephone silence and told myself that Isabel was safe in the hospital, being looked after. No one dies of having a baby nowadays, even if things go wrong. In a few days she'd be home.

I could smell the hospital, as if I were there too. I saw Isabel flat out on one of those trolleys, her face knocked sideways by pain and her eyes closed. Her stomach was hollow where they'd taken out the baby. Her womb had gone too, that grown-up thing that bled three years before mine did. The wheels squeaked and two men shoved her down the corridor, very fast. In the doorway behind, dwindling, Richard watched too. I knew how he would look angry, and helpless.

"I'll come down," I said. "I can be there in less than three hours."

"There's no point in you coming now. I'd planned to have this week off anyway. But I'm in Korea next week, and she'll need someone then. She'll only just be out of hospital."

My mouth opened to ask him if he could cancel the trip to Korea, then shut again. Richard is an economist who specializes in developing computerized models for fast-growth economies. There not much work for him in Europe. Apparently he is accomplished, single-minded, and indispensable in his field. I haven't heard this from Isabel, who never talks about Richard's work, but from an article in the *Financial Times,* which said that if Maynard Keynes were reborn now he would be Richard.

"Of course I'll come. I'll come whenever Isabel needs me."

"Good."

My hands shook as I jabbed the phone's aerial down into its skull and put it on its rest. I had a pain in my throat, as if talking to Richard had hurt me. I found I was clutching my towel tightly round me. Deliberately, I unclenched my fingers and let it fall. There was my stomach, pale and whole. I thought of Isabel's brown summer belly, her deep navel. I touched my skin and ran my hand across it to feel that it was unscarred. Then I went straight into the kitchen, cut a thick crust of a fresh white loaf, smeared it with butter and then with apricot jam, and ate it fast, cramming it into my mouth. There was sweat on my forehead, so I wiped it off and kept on eating. I was not going to let myself think of the things Richard had said, not yet.

It's nearly a mile up the track from the road to Isabel's house. By now I'm walking more slowly, prolonging the moment of not having arrived yet. Usually I do this because I find that holding myself back from something I long for only adds to the pleasure I get in the end. But this time the reason is different. I'm afraid I'll make a mistake. Say the wrong thing, touch her when she doesn't want to be touched, admire the baby when all she cares about is the other babies, the ones she can't have anymore. I can be clumsy sometimes. Richard makes me feel that I am clumsy most of the time. There is too much of me for him.

And then I see it. An owl, its wings spread, going down the lane in front of me. So light, it reminds me —

The way some birds fly, you'd think they were fucking the air.

Who said that? I can't remember. Someone I didn't expect to have thoughts like that, because I was surprised.

The owl will get there first. I shift my case to the other hand yet again, and plod on.

chapter *two*

BUT WHEN I get there, Isabel's asleep. Richard is outside on the broad stone step, sitting on a kitchen chair,
a glass of beer in his hand. I see him first not even as a
person but as a bulk in the summer gloom, barring the
entrance to the house. I get closer and the shadows re-
solve into Richard, like a puzzle picture. There's his
paper collapsed into a tent beside the chair.

"She's asleep," he says as soon as he sees me. "Better
wait till morning now. I didn't think you were coming
so late."

"I had to see someone. It went on longer than I expected." As usual I'm aware of how feeble my world
seems when Richard's cuts across it. He believes that
any meeting lasting longer than an hour is a waste of
time.

"I saw that picture of yours," he says abruptly. "In
the *Telegraph,* wasn't it?"

"The magazine," I say, too quickly.

"Interesting subject."

It was a gypsies' wedding over in Ireland, and I had been there with someone who knew the bridegroom. I'd felt out of place at first, with the drinking and dancing. I don't drink when I'm working, and I don't dance either, or not often, not easily. I knew no one there, not even the man who'd brought me, really, but I got talking to some children, a crowd of them sitting on the steps of a trailer. They wanted to look at the camera, the way kids always do. I had a Polaroid with me too, and that made things easy. Even these days, people often don't want their photos taken, or else they want something back for it, money or other things. I liked that wedding, and it showed in the pictures. I liked the way they'd spent money they hadn't got, and the children were wise to what was going on, the drinking and the fights breaking out, but loving it too, innocently, in the way children can do two things at once. There was a little girl who held out her hand to me for money, and one of the other girls slapped her hand down because I'd given each of them their photograph to keep already. She didn't slap her hard, just a little slap to show she knew what manners were. I took out a ten-pound note and folded it small and wrapped her hand round it, and the big girl said she'd make sure her mammy kept it for her.

"It was good," says Richard. "Good composition."

I smile in the dark. Normally I don't like it when people who don't know the subject use its terminology, but tonight I'm touched that he bothered to notice the picture and tell me that it was good. It seems a good omen.

Behind us the house is silent. "Where's the baby?"

"He's with Susan. Oh, I forgot, you probably don't know about Susan. Susan Wilkinson. She's just finished her nanny course and she can help Isabel out for a couple of months. She's sleeping here the first couple of weeks, but once Isabel's better she'll come every day and sleep at home. Just as well. She's getting on my nerves already."

"Is she good with the baby?"

"She's very good."

We say "the baby" as we did before he was born. He has a name, but to me it doesn't sound like a baby's name. He is called Antony. Much later, when it can't possibly sound like a criticism, I'll ask Isabel how they came to choose it.

"I'll go in," I say. He looks up but only moves aside half a foot or so, and I have to step round him, into the kitchen, which smells old and cool and slightly fusty, as if it's a long time since anyone's cooked here. I pull the string and the light comes on. It's a big room, floored in stone, with a few dirty rag rugs that were here before Isabel came. Then there's an electric stove, which looks too small for the room, and cupboards, lots of cupboards, in which there are sometimes mouse droppings.

There is a square table marked by knives, on which there's a heap of gooseberries in a wooden colander. A woodstove that is never used crouches against one wall. The Wilkinsons lived here in the farmhouse once, before they made enough money selling a hundred acres when land prices were high to build themselves the house of their dreams, two fields away. Once I thought I'd like to make a collage from images of these two houses, like two hands of cards dealt together, but then I knew it would be too easy, and too obvious. Mrs. Wilkinson has a fitted kitchen in pale buffed oak. She has good taste.

I love this room. To me it seems entirely beautiful, in the same way as my sister seems entirely beautiful, and yet it makes me angry. I almost don't want to see it. If this is beautiful, if it calls out in me that small almost sexual shiver I can't fake, then what does that say about my white-walled attic flat with its windows set in at odd angles, showing other people's chimney pots and tiles. I could no more make a kitchen like Isabel's than I could fly through the air.

Isabel doesn't own the house. She has it on a lease from the Wilkinsons, who sometimes speak of how they'll do it up for their sons when they marry. I've seen Margery Wilkinson drink her cup of tea in here and look round appraisingly at a window to be double-glazed, or a row of shelves to be torn out. But Isabel lives here as if she'll live here forever. That was why she wanted to have the baby in this house, upstairs, in her own bed, so that he'd first open his eyes here. I suppose Richard might want to buy a house, but Isabel won't leave here until she's forced out. He must have known that when he married her.

Richard comes in, yawning. He throws the paper on the table and takes a bottle of whisky out of a cupboard, and two small glasses. I shake my head. It's one of the few drinks I don't like.

"You might as well," he says. "There's not much chance of a decent night's sleep otherwise."

"Does he cry a lot?"

"I don't know what they're supposed to do, but he seems to cry most of the night, yes. And then there's Susan pattering about in her pajamas, so it's hardly restful. She sees no reason why I should sleep while she and Isabel are awake."

I take the offered glass. He pours whisky in, not too much, and again I'm pleased. The whisky tastes disgusting, as usual. He pours himself another immediately.

"That bloody girl's got religion as well," he says.

"What, Susan?"

"Mm. She went off to some Jesus camp in the summer, and she's never stopped talking about it since. God help the children she gets her hands on. She's going to be a nanny, you know."

"Well, you don't need to worry about the baby yet."

"No, I suppose not. But it's a bore for Isabel . . ." He frowns. "On top of the baby and everything else."

I look at him. At that moment I realize that I've been wrong all the time, ever since Isabel first told me she was pregnant. It was an accident, she said, her lids half-closed, smiling slightly. She sounded unworried, but cool, and of course I believed her. I'm in the habit of believing Isabel's version. It was as deliberate a composition as a photograph of a begging child, alone on a barren street, carefully angled to exclude the mother three yards away. It wasn't Richard who had wanted the baby, it was Isabel. What Richard wanted was their life together as it had been before, with no extra presences forced on them. First Susan Wilkinson, and now me. And the baby. He'll do his best for the baby because that's the kind of man he is, but he would have preferred to be alone with Isabel. He doesn't mind that there will be no more children.

I know how he feels, because it is how I feel myself.

I hold out my glass, and he pours in more whisky. The whisky burns a hole in my stomach, as sun through a magnifying glass burns into grass on a hot day. I lean back against the wall and the alcohol skids into my veins.

"You'll see her in the morning," Richard goes on, unfolding the paper, refolding it with the pages in the right order. "I'll be off at six, so I shan't see you."

"Oh."

"Tell Susan I'm back on Friday. I've cut the trip short. She might have forgotten, she's a bit dozy. I've given her a list of phone numbers to pass on to you. Any problem, ring me."

"Of course I will," I say, too quickly, too airily, for he slaps me down.

"I mean it. If she's not well again, don't start thinking you can cope. Get on to me right away." He is massive, more adult and more experienced than I can ever be. But he sways slightly, his head down, like an animal being baited by something just out of sight.

On the other side of this cold wall there's a corridor, and then a staircase, and at the top there are seven doors. Behind one of them there's Isabel, sleeping now. Their bedroom with its smell of marriage that vanishes as soon as Richard goes, and becomes the smell of Isabel again. Her skin, her hair, her oatmeal soap in her bedroom washbasin, and the clothes she's taken off hanging on the back of the door. She wears one scent all the time, and although I like it myself I would never buy it. I've sprayed it on myself in department stores sometimes, and for a few seconds I've become someone else. Not quite Isabel. I'm bad at scents and makeup, bad at clothes. It took me years to realize that it might be easier to do things like shave my legs or make an appointment at a good hairdresser's than not to do them. It's always seemed so complicated to me, being a woman. I hear other women talking about "my size" and "what suits me," swapping tales of smears and tests and samples. I'd like to be that confident. I'd like to believe those things were part of me, and I was part of them. Maybe that's why it suits me to take pictures. No one looks at the person behind the camera.

But I did a series of self-portraits once. It was hard to begin with, but it got easier. In one I was naked. Not naked the way I'd want anyone else to see me, not posing naked or sex naked. Just naked. It was a strange thing to do, and at the time I had no idea why I was doing it. But it worked. All the things that make me uneasy broke down into grains of black and white. What I needed to think about was the technicalities. In the end I quite liked looking at those shapes, those angles, and what the light had done. I did justice to my own flesh and blood.

I wonder if Isabel's really asleep.

chapter *three*

I'M AWAKE at five. I want to pee but I hear Richard moving about, water rushing, doors opening and closing, then a thin, startled sound that I don't identify straightaway. Of course, the baby. It cries hectically, then suddenly stops. The light is soft and gray. I've left my curtains open. This side of the house doesn't look out over Isabel's garden, but over the pond and the barns. A family of ducks sails out, the ducklings bobbing with minute confidence in their mother's wake. There's gray dew on the grass, except where the ducks have walked and left their trail.

A door slams downstairs. Richard, going. I hear his footsteps crunch round to the patch of gravel where they keep their car. I lean out, feeling the cool on my arms, still wanting to pee. The car door clunks, the engine turns, the tires spit gravel, and he's gone. I listen for a long time to the whine of the engine going down the track slowly, in second gear.

I step out into the corridor. There's no sign of Susan

and no sound of the baby now. Isabel's door is closed. I go into the bathroom, where a huge mahogany-seated lavatory squats by the bath. I pee quietly, and pull the long chain. Water roars over the crazed porcelain, sluicing the name Victrix. Water seethes in the cistern, and then silence replaces noise again. They must all be asleep. I look at my watch. Five past six.

I wash my face and hands in cold, chalky water, then creep back to the bedroom, pull on my jeans and the red tank top I've washed out and dried overnight. It's damp, but that feels nice. It's going to be hot again. There is heat everywhere this summer, rolled up overnight like a blanket. I could go out. To the garden, perhaps, to see how it's changed since I was here last time. Or through the farmyard onto the thread of a path that leads to the Downs. But I'm here to look after Isabel, who may be sleeping or may be lying flat on her back, staring out of the window, a single vertical line cut into her forehead. That line comes when she has pain. I step back into the corridor, tasting its cool, smooth boards with my bare feet.

"Nina? Nina, is that you?"

Our mother wouldn't let us shout from room to room. "If you want to say something to Isabel, go and find her first." I remember staring in wonder at a schoolfriend who bawled "Mu-um! I'm home!" as she opened the front door. If we wanted to speak to our mother, we could go in and speak to her. We rarely did. The door of her studio was shut, and behind it she was working. If we went in she would glance up, her slippery hands controlling the live clay by touch, and most of the things we were going to say would seem not worth saying.

"Nina?"

I open the door. There she is, sitting up in bed. "Isabel!"

"Come on in, darling. Shut the door or I'll have Susan back again." She smiles, putting the paper she's writing on to one side, but keeping the pen in her hand. She's got her reading glasses on, the wire-rimmed ones she got in a secondhand shop. She can see through them perfectly, she says. I go up to the bed, feel myself smiling down at her, a big, speechless smile that stretches wider and wider until I don't know what to do with it. Isabel holds out one hand and lifts her face to be kissed, shutting her eyes. I kiss her gingerly, on the cheek. She's smooth and warm as always, but I'm afraid to jolt her and start up the pain that I know is hidden somewhere under the bedclothes. She opens her eyes and screws up her nose.

"That wasn't much of a kiss. Lovely top, Nina. You ought to wear colors like that more, instead of all that black."

I glance down at what she's writing. Three or four

sheets of it, closely covered. She sees me looking and says, "I was writing to Edward. He's coming to stay the day after tomorrow. He and Alex have had another bust-up."

I stare at Isabel. "Hasn't he got more sense than to come here now, when you're still ill? Who does he think's going to look after him?"

She smiles and shrugs. "You know Edward. He doesn't take much looking after. He just wants to get away for a while and try to work out what to do. I had a long letter from him yesterday."

"Does Richard know?"

"Of course."

When I first came in I thought she looked well, but now I can see how pallid she is under her usual summer tan. Isabel doesn't easily show tiredness, or illness. She shifts her legs under the cotton cover.

"I'm supposed to keep doing these exercises," she explains, "to stop getting blood clots. It's lucky no one tells you about all this beforehand. I shouldn't tell *you*." There's this fiction between us that I might start wanting children someday.

"Is it all healing up okay?" I ask cautiously. Isabel laughs.

"Don't worry, Neen, I'm not going to show you. It's not as bad as you'd think. The midwife says I'm a good healer."

When she was pregnant Isabel talked about the midwife a lot. *Midwife* sounds like a word that ought to be archaic, but isn't. I imagined her earthy, full of wisdom, her eyes kind, her hands cool, her hair streaked with gray: the way Isabel wanted her to be, perhaps. But I met her once, and she was a wispy fair girl driving a Ford Fiesta. Isabel and I were in the habit of exaggerating our own lives, and each other's. I was London, a series of small flats with someone living below who played "Do You Really Love Me?" with the speakers hanging out the windows, and my phone ringing at midnight. I was work and safe sex but lots of it and cruising the streets for a late-night pharmacist, and crises and spending too much money, and being dissatisfied. What Isabel was took longer to explain. All this began as a game we played, the kind of game sisters play when they need to find out how different they are. But it turned into a game that played us.

"I don't mind if you show me," I say.

Isabel raises her eyebrows. She pushes down the cover, and pulls up her nightdress. "They've just taken off the dressing and the clips," she says. She's right, it's not as bad as I'd imagined. The scar is a reddish-purple line, with what look like rows of teethmarks above and below it. "That's where the clips were," says Isabel, "and that's where they put in the drain." She looks down at her scar, absorbed. "They keep going on about how I'll still be able to wear a bikini."

Her pubic hair has been shaved off and there are deep bruises on her stomach. "The things they think of," she says.

"What's he like?"

A secretive expression crosses Isabel's face. I know it well. She always looked like this when she first made a new friend whom she didn't want me to meet. "Not at all what I expected," she says. "You'll see."

"I can't wait to see him."

"It's wonderful when he's asleep. Susan's taken him because it's too light in here. He thinks it's morning. But I'll have to feed him again at seven." She frowns and pushes her glasses back up her nose.

"Just tell me what you want doing. I've come to help."

Isabel's face lightens. "Oh, Neen, I've been thinking about it half the night. You know I'd put in three new apple trees in that bed at the bottom of the south wall? Richard won't have watered them, and they need gallons in this weather. Could you run the hose down there and let them soak?"

"Of course," I say. And then, "It's a pity Richard took the car. I could easily have driven him to the airport, and then we'd have had it while he was away."

"I didn't even think of it," says Isabel. "I keep for-getting you can drive." I can drive, Isabel can't. I learned five years ago when I started getting commis-sions that meant travel.

"It's only a mile and a bit into the village as the bee flies," says Isabel.

"Not as the pram pushes," I point out.

"He won't be in a pram. I've got a sling."

"But you've *got* a pram, haven't you?" That was one of my plans, that I'd take the baby for long walks in his pram while Isabel slept. I've never pushed a real pram, and I quite liked the idea of it.

"I haven't bothered. Where would Susan push it, down the track and back again? We'll sort out some-thing once Richard gets back."

But she has piles of clothes, collected here and there, plain white nightgowns and hand-knitted cardigans. She has even embroidered tiny ducks and apples on them herself. When I was here last I watched her em-broider, a new skill for her long, quick fingers.

Isabel leans back suddenly. "I'm so tired," she says suddenly, in a voice wrenched from some place she re-fuses to show me.

"I'll go. I'll let you sleep."

"Don't go yet." She shuts her eyes. They shut tight, the lids sealed over the globes of her eyes. Her face is thinner, but her breasts are round and hard as stones under the thin lawn of her nightdress. The pen she's dropped is staining the bedcover. Without saying anything I pick it up, and the sheets of paper. *Richard feels* . . . I read. I put the papers on her bedside table.

"Can I get you anything?"

Her head moves on the pillow, side to side, slowly. No. One of her hands creeps toward me, an inch or two, palm upturned. I take it and fold it in mine.

"I'll just sit here, then," I say quietly, and I think she smiles. I sit still, holding Isabel's hand. Her bed is placed so that someone sitting up looks straight out over the garden, and then beyond the garden wall to the meadows and the line of the Downs. I can see a tree with red fruit on it that seems to drip down the stone of the wall. There are cattle moving into one of the meadows, a long line of them, seeming to go by themselves at this distance. But then I hear a faint cry through the window, a man's voice, driving the cattle. And another cry, not faint at all, answering it from inside the house. The baby. Even on me it acts like sandpaper jagging over my skin. I feel Isabel tense. I look down and see two rings rise like jumping fish, one over each nipple. Her milk. She turns and opens her eyes, begins to raise herself awkwardly on one elbow.

"Tell Susan to bring him in. I don't want him to cry."

*   *   *

Next to Isabel, Susan looks indecently healthy. Her short fair curls brush Isabel's cheek as she leans down with the baby, putting him with what looks like exaggerated care into Isabel's arms. He is purple all over, arms and legs wagging feebly as he feels himself let down through the air. He butts into Isabel and screams.

"He can smell the milk," says Susan in a loud voice. A fight breaks out between Isabel's breast and the baby, who doesn't seem to know what to do with it. "He's not latched on! He's not latched on!" shouts Susan.

"All *right*," says Isabel in a low, furious voice. The baby dives toward her navel, his head wobbling. The struggle begins again, the baby screaming louder than ever, Susan forcing his head up, a film of sweat appearing on Isabel's forehead. Suddenly there is silence.

"Jesus Christ," says Isabel. The baby sucks noisily, his purple color draining to pink. Susan stands back, and slowly Isabel's free hand comes around the baby, and her two middle fingers begin to tap his back.

"Ooh, we've started him off on the wrong side, I never realized," says Susan.

"Well he's not bloody coming off now," says Isabel with her eyes shut.

"Shall I make you a cup of tea?" I suggest. I catch a glint of a glance from Isabel.

"Susan'll make it. She knows where everything is,"

she says firmly, and Susan goes off with a crisp, bright tread that somehow manages to be reproachful too.

"It's not like that when she's not here," says Isabel.

"It looked . . ." I fumble for the right words. "Extra-ordinary."

Isabel laughs. "Have a proper look at him now she's gone. Do you like him?"

I look at him. Now he is calm I can see he's fair. He even has a light lick of hair. His eyes are screwed shut.

"He's such a big baby. I thought he'd be tiny and dark," says Isabel.

Tiny and dark, like I was. Isabel can remember that.

"He doesn't look much like Richard," I say.

"No," says Isabel, but she's only half listening now. One finger touches the sole of a dangling purple foot, which kicks convulsively. She looks inward, and re-mote. I remember suddenly how she would take my baby out of the doll's pram we shared, in order to lay hers there.

"I want you to take pictures of him," she says.

chapter *four*

I'M UNDER the fig tree, with its big leaves all round me like hands to keep off the sun. There are plenty of figs this year, and for once they're going to ripen. Their warm, spicy smell fills the shade where I sit. It's half-past two, and the sky's white with heat. In this weather you sit out the glare, waiting for the long light of evening. But I don't mind, not here, not miles from London, where the only sound of traffic is the distant hoot of a train as it gets to the crossing, and there's no one crowding into my shade. The shadow of the fig leaves is extraordinarily sharp, almost more distinct than the thing itself. I put out my foot, let the edge of shadow cut it, draw it back again.

From here you can't see the house, and the house can't see you. Or rather, no one in the house can see me now. I count them up. Susan, in her glory this afternoon because the health service visitor is coming at three. Isabel, who must be there too. Edward, who lay in bed most of the morning, recovering, and has probably gone back there again after eating a good lunch. Recovering from what? Too much sex between the wrong people, that's all it comes down to, though he and Isabel have turned it into something else, which puts out its feelers all over the house. Every time I come into a room there he is, Edward, moody on a footstool, his chin on his hands, explaining to Isabel the enigma that is himself. He stops when he sees me. Edward has an actor's instinct for a good audience.

Susan's scented danger. Edward is a serious distraction from the business of baby. She tried sending him off on a mission to get a particular type of baby cream yesterday, and even had a small list made out for him of things he might as well get while he was there. Edward doesn't drive, either, so this involved two changes of bus. It would have kept him out of the house for several hours. Edward didn't say no. He never says no. He smiled at Susan, and waited until she went away again.

The baby sleeps. That baby sleeps with his whole heart. I'm getting to like watching him, the patterns he makes across his white flannelette sheets, the way he flings himself down the current of sleep, his lips pursed, his face so smooth there seem to be no features in it at all. Or perhaps just the perfect dab of his nose, at some angles. I look at him for a long time, but I haven't taken any pictures yet, or tried to draw him. It's hard to get in to see him alone. He is Isabel's. I don't want to draw the curve of her arm around him, or the way her neck bends, or his legs curling to her breast. He's often naked while she feeds him, because it's so hot. Isabel's offering me these things all the time, but I don't want them. I know them already.

And of course there's more to it than that. Of course I'm jealous. But of whom?

I've brought out a sketchbook. Just a little one, the paper the size of a postcard. That's the kind of drawing I want to do, drawings done as if through a keyhole, so that the way the image is framed becomes as important as the image itself. But my eye's out. I don't draw enough. You have to draw every day, every single day, if you want to keep your eye in. And your hand, and all the other things. My mother was the first person who taught me to draw. When I got angry with myself and crumpled things up she'd say, "It doesn't matter. Better to do a drawing than not do one, even if it's no good. Because of that bad drawing you'll be able to do a better one tomorrow." She had no time for people who wanted everything they did to be perfect. I can remember it now, sitting in her studio facing the tumble of roofs above the beach. Only it wasn't a tumble once you looked at it. Every roof related precisely to space and the tilt of the land. I can hear her say, "You have to *look* at it, Nina." And then her hand came over my shoulder, she took a piece of paper, drew quickly.

"That's only the way I see it," she said. Her hands were long like Isabel's, but much rougher. You could see she worked with her hands. "In fact I think you'll draw better than I do, in the end, if you keep at it."

I'm going to draw that cabbage, there, that fat loose one squatting in a bed of big poppies. I'm going to do it quickly, without thinking about it too much. I flip to a new page, hold my pencil like a cutting tool, and begin.

He doesn't surprise me. When you're looking so hard, you notice every change of light, and his shadow is big, like him. He's still in a suit.

"I thought I'd find some shade here," he says. "You don't mind if I join you?"

I move along the wooden bench, closing the sketch-book. "No, of course not."

"I've stopped you working," he says. "I didn't want to do that."

I glance up, pleased and surprised. "I'll go back to it," I say. "Is the health visitor still there?"

"I haven't been in yet," says Richard.

He looks tired, his dark skin sallow. "There was a crowd of them in the bedroom," he says. "I'll go in to Isabel once she's alone. I rang from the airport."

"Edward's here."

"Yes, I thought he very probably would be."

"Alex might be coming down at the weekend too."

Richard doesn't answer. He stares out over the garden, his eyes narrowed against the glare.

"And here you are drawing a cabbage," he says.

"I'm perfectly happy," I say, and it's true.

He turns and looks at me, then says, "I've never seen it before, but you do look like your mother, don't you? There's a photo of her working that looks like you did just then."

"You never saw my father, either."

"No. I'd like to have met him. Isabel was very fond of him."

"He was very selfish," I say suddenly, without meaning to. "I didn't realize it until he was dead. It was impossible to think that while you were with him. "

"Isabel says your mother was selfish. Before she had the baby, she said all she'd have to do was think of what your mother did with you two, and then do the opposite."

He looks at me closely. I wonder if we are talking about my parents still, or about me and Isabel. "I know she thinks that," I say, "but it would have been different if she'd been interested in what my mother did."

"You say 'my mother.' So does Isabel. Not 'our mother.' "

"We see her differently."

Part of me itches for him to go, so I can pick up the

pencil again. I can see another, better way of drawing the cabbage now. But on the other hand, this is the least awkward conversation I've ever had with Richard.

"The baby looks a bit like him," I say abruptly.

"Who?"

"My father. Our father. His grandfather," I say, discovering this fact suddenly. The baby is not just Isabel's. It is knitted into a chain of resemblances.

"It amazes me how people find resemblances in babies," says Richard.

"I suppose it's what you look for."

He frowns, as if impatient. He wants to be with Isabel, not here. He's counting the moments until he hears the health visitor's car go down the track, until he can see Isabel on his own.

"I'm starving," he says. "The food on the plane was inedible."

"There's some gooseberry pie in the fridge."

"You couldn't get me some, could you, Nina? I don't want to bump into that woman."

"Well . . . ," I say, my hand reaching for the sketchbook, which I am not going to leave with him, "all right."

He smiles, his eyes going into their creases. Richard is forty-six, older, heavier, weightier than Isabel or I. "Good," he says. I stand up and walk out of the shade into the glare of the sun, up one of Isabel's little paths.

She has planted low box hedges to contain the profusion that loops through trees, over trellises, up walls, and around doorways. I like that dark, firm green. I like the way these hedges pinch the sense that there is too much of everything here. It's very like Isabel, who is beautiful enough to wear reading glasses that most women would throw away.

I find the pie under a plate. Edward has been at it since lunch, digging out the fruit, which he prefers to the crust. I cut a straight line across the spoiled part, and then a thick wedge, the right size for Richard. There's some cream in a jug, thick and yellow. Susan's mother sent the pie over, and it has a spray of elder-flower in it to bring out the taste of the gooseberries. She has patterned the crust with pastry leaves. The inside of the crust is white and glutinous now the pastry has cooled, and cooking has thinned the skin of the berries so the seeds show through. I pick one out, fragile but still whole, and eat it. I am hungry too. I cut another piece of the pie, for myself, and pour cream over them both, take two spoons and shake some sugar from a cas-tor over the cream. I can hear voices, but the baby has stopped crying. A door opens and the voices grow louder. They must be coming out. I pick up the plates and hurry out into the light, round the corner by the pond, and into the garden.

Richard hasn't moved, except to take off his shoes

and socks. He lies back with his feet in the sun, eyes shut. His feet are pale, naked-looking city feet.

"Here you are."

We dig into the crust, the cream, the fruit. The edges of the cream are just beginning to swim in the heat already. I've always liked eating with Richard, because he is greedy, as I am. You can always tell. He leaves the plumpest gooseberry until last, to duck it in its own pond of cream. The sugar grits pleasantly on my teeth.

"I should have brought the rest of it," I say. "Edward'll only eat it otherwise."

Wasps are on the empty plates already. "Better go in," says Richard, weighing, picking up his shoes.

"I didn't hear the car leave."

"Didn't you? I did. You were lost in that pie."

"I'll come later," I say. The cabbage has changed slightly, wilted a little in the afternoon heat.

"If she stood at the window, and I stood on the path, just by those sweet Williams, I could see her," says Richard. "She often looks at the garden from there."

"She hasn't been out. It's too hot for the baby."

"He'll have to get used to it," says Richard. "Isabel lives in this garden."

But she hasn't been in it since I got here. Edward doesn't like the sun, either, and their long talks go on indoors, in Isabel's room, or in the shaded, stuffy downstairs sitting room. I couldn't have imagined the garden

39

without Isabel before this summer. She knew it, she planted it, she was always moving in it somewhere, or else she'd have left a trowel, a tray of cuttings, a ball of string to show that she'd be back soon. But the garden goes on without her, though I know it's an illusion. It'll rot from the inside, like pears left too long in a bowl.

But it's perfect now, and this afternoon it feels as much mine as anyone's. I move back deeper into the shade of the fig tree. I think I'll draw one of the unripe fruit next, the bare knob of it stuck to its silvery branch. Everything around me seems to have grown on its own, flaring into color or fading like those delphiniums, which are bleached ghosts of themselves now. Drawing is easier when I can't see Isabel's long hands everywhere, in the soil, among the leaves, parting clumps of flowers, cutting, nicking, grafting, taking away.

chapter five

"YOU DON'T LOOK very alike," Susan said yesterday. "I wouldn't have guessed you were sisters."

She had the baby in her arms. He'd been miserable all day after crying half the night, and Isabel was exhausted. The wound wasn't healing where the drain had been, Susan said. She was going to phone the doctor later. Isabel was resting while Richard sat with her in the big armchair, going through papers. I had cooked a chicken to eat cold for supper, and dug up new potatoes. They'd been white as eggs when they came out of the earth, but they were skinning over now, already brown. Later, just before we ate, I'd pull some lettuce.

"I like those shorts," said Susan. "I think it's nice, the way everyone wears shorts now."

I looked down at my legs, and laughed. They were far from perfect, but I liked them.

"She's beautiful, isn't she?" said Susan, staring at me intently as if she really didn't know the answer.

"Yes, she is," I answered, and Susan sighed.

"Never mind," I said. "We don't all have to look like that."

She grinned back. For the first time we were nearly liking each other. "I haven't got a sister," she said, "just brothers. Great lumps playing at cricket the whole time. Everyone's mad about cricket round here."

"There were just the two of us," I said.

"Yes, but you were the artistic one, weren't you?" she went on, following a train of thought that led from Isabel's beauty.

"I take photographs, and I draw. I don't call myself an artist."

"You do lovely drawings. I've always wanted to be able to draw." As she said it I saw her as a little girl, leaning breathily over the shoulder of a schoolfriend. "Ooh, yours is brilliant! Mine's rubbish." But I couldn't be bothered to give Susan the contradictions she wanted. I smiled vaguely and wiped my earthy hands on my shorts.

I keep thinking about Isabel. Being in the same house for so long is working strangely, making me think of her more rather than less. I think of our being sisters. She's like me, more like me than Susan sees, and yet not like. All those genes thrown up into the air as casually as dice have come down quite differently each time. Once I used to think Isabel had had all the sixes, but now I'm not so sure. She's three years older than me, so the family she grew up in was never quite the same as the one I knew. She remembers — or says she remembers — the time before I was born, when she walked between our parents holding a hand of each, linking them. When she talked to our parents about that time in front of me, I seemed to vanish. My not existing was as real to them as my existing. Isabel remembers our mother being pregnant. She was the big one, the sensible one, and I was the toddler who could scream and bite. For years I accepted Isabel's lists of the things I had done to her, not even beginning to think that there might be other lists, other things, done to me. She told her stories with an air of adult patience, for adult ears.

"Nina cut the eyelashes off Rosina. She thought they'd grow again. She doesn't realize Rosina's only a doll."

But she doesn't tell how every time it was my turn for the doll's pram she would calmly, firmly take out my doll and put in her own.

"You see, Nina, Mandy doesn't fit in the pram properly. Look at her legs sticking out. Rosina came with the pram, so it's hers really. But I'll let you have a turn pushing her."

And off we went to push our doll's pram round Barnoon Cemetery, up and down the little paths, visiting our favorite graves. Below us the sea glittered and the holiday people threw themselves in and out of the waves, but we took no notice of them. Our parents let us go where we liked. We'd walk as far as Wicca Pool sometimes, and swim with the seals. Once we saw a honeymoon couple bathing there naked, their fronds of pubic hairs touching.

"They'll lie down on the rocks and cuddle each other next," said Isabel authoritatively, and they did. Isabel was so sure of things that sometimes I thought it was her certainty that made them happen. Without Isabel's predictions I'd have been lost in a world where anything might come next. She even knew when I was going to cry.

Once I slipped when we were running back along the cliff path. We'd been picking blackberries and I was watching the berries bounce in the bucket clasped in front of me, not the path. My foot caught on a stone, and I fell sideways, not safely onto the path, but sliding with horrible smoothness and speed to the lip of the cliff. I saw myself going and heard Isabel scream, then I went over. But it was a rough slope, not the edge of the cliff itself, which was still fifteen feet away. I slid ten of them, bumping and banging, then stopped. I began to scream, lying on my back, looking straight up at the sky. A second later a half circle of terror broke the sky, upside down. It took me a moment to realize that this was Isabel's face. The next minute she was with me, dragging me back with both hands over the scattered blackberries. I got back to the path and sat down on it, shivering. My legs were smeared with blood and blackberry juice. There was a long, burning graze up the inside of my arms.

"My bucket's gone," I said.

"I'll have a look." Isabel stood up and peered down. "I can't see it. It must have gone over."

I thought of my new bucket, silvery inside, bouncing and clanging down to the rocks, and I began to cry. Then Isabel was crying too, worse than me, shaking and hiding her face with her hands. She hardly ever cried, and this was worse than losing the bucket. I patted her shoulders, but she didn't seem to feel it. "It's all right, Isabel. I didn't fall. I'm all right." But she cried harder, and I gave up and began to pick up the fallen blackberries and eat them. I wiped off the dust carefully and popped them into my mouth, one by one. They were delicious. And then there was Isabel, facing me on hands and knees, her face fierce. She was all smeary with crying, but back to herself again.

"And don't you dare tell them, Nina. Or I'll say I told you to stop and you ran on."

I wonder what Isabel sees when she looks back at the past. We aren't the kind of sisters who talk about their

45

childhood together. If we did we might find we hadn't got many shared memories. And here's Antony, who won't have a brother or a sister at all. No one to cover up for, and no one to betray. Isabel hasn't talked about that. She showed me the scar, but she hasn't talked about what the hysterectomy means to her. Now that there are no more baby clothes to embroider she spends hours doing a cross-stitch landscape, while Edward talks to her. I can see Edward loving it: the dip of Isabel's head, the maternity he can enjoy when the baby's not there, the needle flashing in and out. Isabel works quickly, and she listens carefully, looking up at him from time to time, letting him talk himself out. Or they are silent together. I don't like it when I come into her room in the middle of one of their silences.

Richard comes into the kitchen while I'm jointing the chicken.

"How's Isabel?"

"She's trying to sleep. She says she can't settle down while I'm there." He pours water into the kettle and plugs it in. "I'm getting that doctor over. She ought to be feeling better than this by now."

I expect him to go straight out with his coffee, but he sits down in one of the high-backed kitchen chairs.

"Can I give you a hand?"

"You could chop these onions and put them in the salad."

"What's that you're making?"

"I'm going to do a chicken risotto for Isabel. She might like something hot, we've had a lot of salad."

"You're a good cook, aren't you?"

"I should be."

"Why?"

"People who like eating make the best cooks."

He smiles. "Have you been drawing again today?"

"Yes, I was out this morning." I say it quickly, like someone hiding a secret greed. "I took some pictures too, over at the Wilkinsons'. But it's not my subject. I don't know enough about farming. They're just snaps. Susan's interesting, though. I'd like to do some pictures of Susan when she's working with the baby."

"I hadn't really looked at her," says Richard. I smile, and cube breast of chicken with one of Isabel's sharp knives.

"Susan's going to be quite something when she gets going," I say.

"Can't you take some pictures of Isabel? I know she wants you to."

"Oh, I expect I will. There's plenty of time."

"It seems a bit of a waste of time photographing

Susan. It's not as if she's going to carry on working here. The baby'll never see her again once she goes off to be a nanny."

"It's what's happening now that interests me," I say. "That's what I draw. That's what I photograph. I don't look at a cabbage and say it's not worth drawing because we're going to eat it tomorrow."

Richard is silent. Then, "I don't care what you do," he says rather irritably. "I was only thinking of Isabel."

"I know you were." I look up from the bowl of fine, moist chicken, and hold his eyes. "I'm here because you asked me to come," I say, "but I'm not just something of Isabel's."

"I didn't think you were," he says, looking straight back at me.

I stand up and go to one of the cupboards behind me. I take out green olive oil, arborio rice, a tiny packet of saffron, pine nuts.

"You've been shopping."

"Yes, I took your car into Lewes this morning. You re-member I asked you if I could use it."

"Of course you can use it. It's ridiculous the way no one drives it but me. But you've got lots of stuff there — how much do I owe you?"

"I'm staying in your house, eating your food all the time. Anyway, I've got plenty of money at the moment."

"Have you? Are things going well?"

"I'm charging more than I was. It's going fine."

It's true. The kind of work I don't really want flows in. Documentary, and a bit banal. One day I got out of the taxi and saw my camera bag still on the floor. I could never afford to replace the stuff. And yet I had to stop myself from paying the fare, turning away, disappearing into the anonymous crowd.

"It's going fine," I repeat. I'm standing as I say this, pouring a thin stream of oil into Isabel's heaviest pan, looking down on him.

"It's important to make sure you charge enough. Other people judge you by that," he says.

"Don't worry," I say. "Money's important to me."

"And to me. But then I'm not an artist."

"Artists don't have to be stupid. My mother wasn't. She was very good with money."

"I want Isabel to approach Wilkinson again, about buying this house. I could make him the kind of offer he'd think twice about. But she's against it."

"It would be your house then," I point out.

"It would be in our joint names."

"Yes. But the lease is in Isabel's name now."

"She doesn't like talking about it. She says I knew the situation when we married, which I did. But situations are fluid, they can change."

This is the first time I've heard Richard say anything remotely critical of Isabel. He's noticed something I thought only I had noticed, that Isabel doesn't like change. She's afraid of it. It's true that she's followed her own path, but having done so she rarely steps off it. And suddenly I feel a wash of tenderness for her, without knowing where this comes from.

chapter six

BEYOND ISABEL'S garden, before the Downs, there are the water meadows. The river runs through them. All day it's been wrapped in the heat-haze that hides the Downs. It's been hot enough for mirages, for rivers walking upside down on air. Isabel says the river is the reason she came here. She was walking along the river, and she saw the house staring at her from its empty windows. She climbed the wall and dropped down into the garden from the branches of a plum tree. Just Isabel, alone in a hot, quiet garden that had been empty so long even the birds weren't afraid of her. Everything was matted with bindweed and brambles, which would take her two years to clear before she began to plant.

Some winters the river floods the meadows, but now it runs smoothly between its banks, which are raised above the land on either side. There is so much chalk in the water that it turns a pale, opaque green in the sun. Isabel says it's full of chemicals washed off the soil, and though children used to swim in it, they can't anymore.

It's one in the morning, and I'm lying in the dark, the curtains open wide, the warm air moving over my skin. I can't sleep, because of the heat, and a homesickness which I'm used to, which has nothing to do with being away from my flat in London. I think of the sea, and the noise of the waves. When I first moved to the city, it took me a while to realize what I was listening for all the time. In London, if I'm half-asleep, I make distant traffic into the snarl of a winter sea. I wish I could hear the river, but it slides silently through the fields, hidden. The current runs deep and strong.

"Neen. Neen."

"Come in."

I pull the sheet over me and sit up. Isabel pushes the door open and comes in.

"Put the light on."

She crosses the floor and switches on the little lamp by the bed.

"I didn't wake you up, did I?"

"No. I was listening for the river."

"You can't hear it."

"I know."

"You can't even see it from here," Isabel says. She goes to the window and looks out. "Do you remember how we used to go out at night, without them knowing?"

"Yes."

"You used to be frightened of how loud the sea sounded in the dark." She yawns, pushes back her hair, rubs the stains of tiredness under her eyes.

"You should be asleep," I say.

"He'll wake in less than an hour. It's hardly worth it."

"You ought to let Susan give him a bottle at night so you can get some sleep. She said she would."

"You bet she would. But she's not going to." Isabel grins. "Let her have her own baby."

She comes back and sits on my bed. "You know, *you* could feed him, Neen," she says. "Did you know that? Women who've never had babies can breast-feed if they keep on letting the baby suck. Some women strap little pouches of milk to themselves when they adopt a baby, with a tube running to their nipple, so he keeps sucking till the real milk comes." She looks at me, smiling, and her hair shines with wisps of light.

"He's not my baby," I say.

"Don't get cross. It's just a piece of information."

The baby is everything. Everything starts in him and circles back to him, and the rest of us are shadows on the outside of the circle. Me, Richard, Susan. I wonder how Richard feels about it.

"You think I put him first," says Isabel.

"It's natural," I say, coolly, lightly. Or so I hope. I feel as if Isabel has just snatched her hand out of mine.

53

"That's a laugh," says Isabel. "I'll tell you something, Neen. When it was happening, when I started bleeding and I saw the midwife's face and then Richard was running to the phone, all I thought was, 'Don't let me die.' I didn't think of the baby. I thought of me. I thought I was going to bleed to death."

"You nearly did."

"I know." She plucks at the ragged end of the bedspread, then asks abruptly, "Neen, do you think about death a lot?"

"Sometimes."

"Richard says he never does."

"He's probably lying."

"But aren't people different? Isn't it frightening, how different they are?" She looks at me intently, and yet I have the feeling she's still holding back from me. Then she says, "Does Richard talk to you?"

I feel myself blush, for no reason, but I answer easily. "Not much. You know he never does."

"No." I'm not sure if her face relaxes slightly or not. "Maybe he will, while you're here. After all, you're my sister. If he can't talk to you, who can he talk to? It'd do him good."

Suddenly I remember something Isabel must have forgotten. A picnic, when I was sixteen. A cool, windy afternoon, and we walked above the railway line to Carbis Bay. Michael was with us, Isabel's friend from London. I was drawing two fishing boats as they wallowed round the point. I had my back to Michael and Isabel, and I'd almost forgotten them, when Isabel said in a high, insistent voice, "You could draw him, couldn't you, Neen? You could draw Michael?"

I didn't want to. I didn't want to break off what I was doing. But they were older, and they wanted something from me, and I rarely felt that Isabel wanted anything I had to give. I began to draw him, sitting against a stone way-marker. He was good-looking in a way Isabel liked then, thin and a bit evasive. The wind tugged at his hair and my paper, but he was easy to draw, and I knew it was coming out well. He got up once to look at what I'd done so far, and after that he became much more interested and began to talk to me, asking me about my drawing and what I was going to do when I left home. I saw why Isabel liked him once his face was lit up with flattering attention and it was all flowing my way. The drawing went better and better. We were talking about him now, the film he wanted to make, the famous actor who had more or less promised to be in it. Isabel had wandered off somewhere. When she came back the sun was out on the sheltered spot where I was drawing, and I'd nearly finished. Michael called to her, "Have a look at this! You should have told me she was really good." Isabel stooped, smiling, and examined what I'd done. Then she looked measuringly at Michael, a long look.

The next day Michael went home, three days early. I thought he'd have taken the drawing, since he'd asked me if he could have it, but he didn't. I found it crumpled on top of the kitchen rubbish, where he must have thrown it.

"You will stay, won't you?" asks Isabel. It seems to echo, as if she's asked the question before.

"I said I'd stay as long as you needed me," I say. "But you're all right, with Susan and Richard, and Edward. I'm not doing much except the cooking. You don't really need me here."

Isabel frowns. The rich, half-hooped upper eyelids drop over her eyes as she looks down. Her long fingers pluck, pluck at the bedclothes. They are thin, and her wrists are oblong, showing their bones. Only her breasts are heavy. "I do need you," she says, not looking at me.

chapter seven

I TOLD SUSAN that there were just the two of us, Isabel and me, and this is what I always say. But there were three.

My brother was born when I was four years old. Like Isabel earlier, when I was born, I was old enough to notice my mother's pregnancy. It seemed endless. For years, it seemed, she ported a hump in front of her, big and tense and white when she was undressed. Her belly button turned inside out, like a mushroom stalk. I touched it, and she jumped and pushed me away. Every afternoon she locked the studio door, went upstairs to her bedroom, and lay down. We were not allowed to make a noise then, or go to her unless one of us hurt ourselves. It was a late pregnancy: my mother was forty-three and hadn't expected to have another child. I don't know whether she wanted it or not, while she was pregnant, because everything is colored afterward by the real presence of the child.

I didn't want it. She was my mother, mine and Isabel's. Why had she chosen to make things worse like this? There wasn't enough money for us two, let alone a baby. That was why our father was away more and more. I knew this because Isabel listened to them talking, and told me.

"What's it like, having a baby?" I asked Isabel, and she wrinkled her nose, remembering. "Noisy," she said at last. We'd both been born in the house, but this time my mother was going to a hospital, because she was older. There were streaks on my mother's stomach now, red and purple as it stretched. I don't remember my father much from that time.

The day the baby was born was fine and hot. Isabel was given a picnic, a pound note, and two boxes of Rowntrees Fruit Gums, and told to take me to the beach for the day. We walked beyond the surfing beach to a little cove of white sand we knew, where we could make a house by draping seaweed over the black rocks, and stick our lemonade bottle in cold sand.

"She'll be pushing it out now," said Isabel, who knew everything about babies. I nodded, humping the canvas picnic bag over my shoulder while she shook a stone out of her sandal. I didn't care about the baby that day, because Isabel was going to let me fish off the rocks with her fishing line for the first time.

Isabel held me tight round the waist as the waves sucked below us. The water was deep here, and dangerous. If we fell in, we knew, we'd be battered against the rocks. We were far out, too far out. My face was sticky with spray, and every time I opened my mouth I tasted salt. The tide was on the turn, surging past our feet. Isabel's hands held me tight as I leaned out to throw the line clear of the rocks, then we sat back in our niche of rock to wait for the tug. A hundred yards away, on safe rock, a man waved his arms at us. His mouth opened and closed, but we couldn't hear anything above the noise of the waves.

"Stupid idiot," said Isabel. "Still, we'd better go back and see if she's had the baby yet."

I don't remember the journey back, only my father, his face suddenly smooth with happiness, telling us it was a boy. He said it over and over, and Isabel and I looked at each other, a quick, furtive look. Then Isabel said, "Oh, a boy. Never mind, Neen," and she knelt down and put her arms round me, mouthing over my head to our father, *"Neen wanted it to be a girl."* I'd wanted nothing, but I hid my face in Isabel's shirt because it was nice to feel her holding me. After a while my father said that he was going to the hospital, and he went.

They called the baby Colin. I thought about him a lot

for the first day, then forgot him. My mother was in hospital for ten days, and that was what I mostly thought about. Isabel put me to bed each night while our father visited the hospital. There must have been other adults around, friends and neighbors, but I only remember Isabel sitting on the linen chest by the bath squeezing shampoo onto my hair and then rubbing it in.

When my mother came back, she had Colin with her. He seemed to be stuck to her all the time, so that whenever I wanted to climb into her lap he was there. She bottle-fed him, because she wanted to get back to work in the studio as soon as possible, and a girl was going to come in every day to look after him. But he fed and screamed, fed and screamed. Once she upset the hot water in which the feeding bottle stood, and it ran over his foot so he screamed more. But when he stopped feeding she lifted him up and held his face against hers. She shut her eyes and whispered things to him that I couldn't hear.

She was tired for a long time, and not well. I remember creeping in very quietly and lying down beside her on the big double bed while she slept. She opened her eyes and saw me and smiled. Then Colin screamed.

"You ought to smack him, then he wouldn't make so much noise," I told her. But she toiled out of bed and heated his milk.

Colin was three months old. Once I heard my parents talking about Isabel. "It's strange that she doesn't bother with him, when you think how wonderful she is with Neen."

Isabel never asked to hold Colin. Sometimes our mother would say, "Here you are, would you like to hold him?" Isabel would let him loll in her lap until he was taken away. Afterward she would hoist me up into her lap, and tell me stories, because she could read and I couldn't. I leaned against her, talking in the baby language we spoke to our dolls. We tended Rosina and Mandy more than ever, rocking them, soothing them, dressing and undressing them. If Colin was in the room we wouldn't even glance at him.

One evening, after we'd gone to bed, we began a game of babies. Isabel took the sheet and laid me in the middle of it, then wrapped it round me tightly, like a shawl. At first I liked it and lay there sucking my thumb and smiling at her, talking baby talk round the thumb. But then that got boring. I began to struggle free of the sheet. I was on my hands and knees, then on my feet in the deep trough in the middle of the bed.

"Naughty baby!" shouted Isabel, laughing, egging me on. I began to jump, bouncing on the mattress until the springs twanged. I jumped and jumped, screaming with excitement at every bounce. Isabel began to jump too, making me bounce twice, once on my jump and once on hers, while her long hair flew round us both. Suddenly the door opened. My mother was at the bed almost before we'd seen her. She grabbed my arm, and Isabel's.

"Shut up!" she shouted. "Shut up! SHUT UP! You've woken him again and I'd just got him to sleep."

Her face glared at us, white and frayed. She looked as if she'd like to kill us. I shrank toward Isabel. Suddenly my mother turned and went out of the room. I think she was afraid of starting to hit us and not being able to stop. We stood silent, listening to Colin's thin, rising howl. Isabel's cheeks were still red with jumping. I began to cry.

"Ssh, Neen!" she said. "Don't make a noise or she'll come back." She got the sheet and wrapped me up in it again. This time I lay passive, staring up at her while she patted me to sleep, the way we patted our dolls.

When I woke up it was morning. Strong light was falling through the half-open curtains onto the linoleum, where Isabel sat cross-legged, reading a book. I wriggled the sheet loose and rolled over. The house was still and quiet, full of sunlight, and Isabel looked up at me, turned down the corner of her page, and smiled.

We must have played for an hour or so. Not dolls this time. I drew pictures, and Isabel made up stories about them. It must have been very early, in spite of the sun, because the house stayed quiet and the baby didn't cry. Suddenly Isabel said, "I'm going to see Colin." I stared at her in surprise, because neither of us ever went in to see Colin in the mornings. Even if we'd wanted to, we knew we mustn't ever wake him up. I remember I had a purple wax crayon in my fist. Isabel opened our door and went out, and I began to draw again. But straight-away she was back. She knelt down opposite me, poked her face close to mine, and announced, "I don't think Colin's very well. You'd better come and have a look, Neen."

She took my hand and led me out onto the landing. Colin slept in the tiny room over the stairs, and his door was open. Isabel pushed me in ahead of her, and I looked through the bars of his drop-sided cot. But there was no Colin there. Instead there was a strange thing. I put my arm through the bars and felt it, and it was solid and cool, like my wax crayon. I looked at Isabel.

"Where's our baby?"

She pointed into the cot. "That's Colin. He's just gone a funny color."

"Oh," I said. I looked again and saw that she was right.

"We'd better go and get dressed," said Isabel, and we went out, closing the door carefully behind us, and back into our bedroom. We didn't make much noise, but something must have woken our mother, because a few

minutes later we heard her padding along to the bathroom. After she'd pulled the chain she went to Colin's
room, and a second later we heard her begin to scream.

That was my brother, who died of cot-death when he
was three months old. Suddenly I wonder if Richard
even knows that there was ever such a person.

chapter *eight*

ALEX CAME DOWN with a salmon yesterday. He'd driven through the night when the motorways were almost empty, with the salmon lying on the backseat. It was hot in the car at midnight, he said. He had music on and the windows open, as if he were driving in another country, not here. He didn't stay long. He talked to Edward for an hour in Isabel's room, and then he ate bread and cheese in the kitchen and drove away again. But Edward looks happier, and the salmon was left for us, lying facedown in the chest freezer. Alex caught it himself. He's on holiday in Scotland, alone, fishing. The fish kept him company on the way down, wrapped in a freezer pack, and now Alex has gone back the five hundred miles, driving back to the rowan trees and the heather, which is just beginning to flush with color. He looked round Isabel's garden as if it wasn't real, and his car keys kept jingling in his hand. He was elsewhere in his mind. I've always liked Alex, and I liked him even more when I saw him come in carrying the salmon like a baby.

Today I'm going to cook. We'll all eat together, in the dark, cool dining room. I'm going to bake the salmon, very slowly, with dill and juniper berries. I'll serve it just warm, with hollandaise sauce, with new potatoes, French beans, a big ripe cucumber that tastes of fruit, not water, and plum tomatoes from Isabel's greenhouse. They're so ripe that they're splitting at the stalk. And then an apple tart, and a gooseberry fool. It'll take most of the day, especially on Isabel's stove. We'll eat at seven, when the baby's been fed and bathed and with luck will sleep for two hours, even three. Richard is in London today, being interviewed by a financial journalist, but he'll be back at five.

This morning I took the fish out of the freezer and unwrapped it. It was a big, lithe, silvery creature, hardly a scale on it damaged. Alex had packed it carefully, with a sprig of heather in its mouth. He had gutted it, and the flaps of its belly lay neatly together, like lips. It would be sweeter in flavor, more intense, less fatty than a farmed animal. He had wiped the blood off it. It lay on its long dish arched a little, as if remembering a leap.

Edward came in as I was spreading a piece of foil loosely over the fish to keep the flies off while it thawed. It should have been muslin, because foil can rub off the scales, but I hadn't thought to buy any when I went shopping earlier.

"Is that for tonight?" he asked, and I nodded.

"Do you want a hand?"

I looked up, thinking quickly. I never give away the jobs I like best, I'm not that sort of cook.

"You can get the dining room ready. Polish the table and dust the chairs. That'll save me a lot of time."

"Okay," he said, surprising me again. "Where's the stuff?"

I found rags for him, and a hardened lump of beeswax polish. Isabel has no dusters. The house is neither clean nor very dirty, and it reminds me of how things were when we were little, with sand choking the washbasin, shells and seaweed behind the kitchen sink, too much rubbish in the tiny bin that my mother lined with newspaper, and dead bluebottles lying for weeks on windowsills until they seemed like friends. Sometimes Isabel pours Jeyes Fluid down her drains, or boiling water onto an ants' nest that is too near the kitchen, as our mother did. When I watch Isabel do these things I am at home, as if something is going on that is beyond liking, beyond even love. There's a way that my mother would lift the corner of a sheet or a blouse to her face and sniff it for damp after she'd brought in the washing. I've made myself stop doing this, but Isabel goes on. She lines her compost bin with newspaper, too, so that the parcel of peelings and eggshells falls apart soggily when I lift it out.

I am smiling, and Edward is looking at me, ready to smile too.

The tart will take longest. I've bought white Normandy butter, pastry flour, three pounds of sharp, sweet Jonagold apples. They are not the right apples, but I won't get better in the tail end of the season, before the new apples come in. They must be cut evenly, in fine crescents of equal thickness, which will lap round in ring after ring, hooping inward, glazed with apricot jam. The tart must cook until the tips of the apple rings are almost black but the fruit itself is still plump and moist. When you close your eyes and bite you must taste caramel, sharp apple, juice, and the short, sandy texture of sweet pastry all at once. No one taste should be stronger than another. The pastry is made, and resting in the fridge. One piece of equipment that Isabel does possess, among her rusty whisks and wooden spoons that smell of onion, is a huge marble slab with a broken edge. I made the pastry on it, cutting the butter into the heaped flour and rubbing it in quickly, lightly, so the paste just held together.

I'm simmering the reduction for the hollandaise sauce. It smells of bay leaf, more than I think it should. I wonder if I should add a second slice of onion, then decide not to. It bubbles and thickens, releasing the spiciness of mace and a sharp vinegar smell. I love making sauces, real sauces that glisten with egg yolks and lump after lump of butter. I strain the reduction, thin it slightly, and begin to whisk in the egg yolks. Now for the stage I like best. I've got a pan of water simmering on an electric coil, but it's still too high, the water bubbling with more energy than it needs. The controls on these coils are crude. I turn it down and the water seems to go to sleep. Up, and it bubbles. I fiddle again, and at last I get what I want. The water squirms, almost unnoticeably alive. I place my bowl of sauce over it and put in the first lump of butter, watch it start to slither, then whisk. I drop in another lump, whisk again, and go on, watching it thicken, checking the heat, making sure the sauce stays smooth as ointment and doesn't curdle. There are twelve lumps of butter to go in. The sauce swallows them all, gleaming, fattening on what I've given it. I let it cook a little longer, still whisking gently. Now it looks right. I dip in a clean wooden spoon and the sauce coats it perfectly.

The last bit is easy. Lemon juice, a touch of salt and pepper. I dip in the wooden spoon again, run my finger over its back, then taste, closing my eyes.

"I bet that's good," says Richard behind me.

I turn and hold out the spoon. "Have some if you want. You're back early."

"It didn't take as long as I thought."

"Did it go all right?"

"Fine. It'll be in next Thursday's *FT*." He's pleased with himself, the man who's been somewhere and done something. He smells of trains. He looks at the fish, ready to cook now, wrapped in its shroud of buttered foil.

"What's that? Alex's salmon?"

"Yes."

He hovers, smiling, and I put the sauce to one side. "It's time to put it in," I say, and lift the salmon. Richard kneels and opens the oven door.

"It's not very hot," he says.

"It doesn't need to be."

The salmon just fits. I have already checked, so I'm not surprised when it slides in by a whisker. The salmon is in the oven, the potatoes ready to boil, the tomatoes in a warm heap on the table, to be cut as late as possible and sprinkled with chopped basil and brown sugar. The beans are waiting in a colander. The tomatoes are intensely red against the damaged surface of the table. Their skins are tough. I'll score them with the point of a knife, dip them in boiling water, and slip them out of their skins.

Richard has left the outside door open, and a bright tongue of sunlight lies on the stone floor. I think of flowers on the table, of a last-minute picking of warm gooseberries and crushing them with a fork, of the cream I've already whipped to fold into them. I think of our seven bodies, mine, Richard's, Isabel's, the baby's, Alex's, Susan's, Edward's. Alex will be back by his river, a halo of flies round his head. The heat is thinner up there, burning the bracken brown and the rowan berries first to orange, then deep red. The waters he fishes are so sweet that when he's thirsty he cups his hands, dips them, and drinks. Isabel is sitting in the rocking chair, rocking back and forward, back and forward, her eyes half-open. The baby is with Susan, visiting her mother. Susan's tied him into a sling and walked him across the fields for tea, his little bare head covered in a denim sunhat. Edward has polished the table and laid it for five of us, and now he's typing a long letter to Alex into his laptop. But it's too hot to think and his fingers slip on the keys. A small plane has gone over twice, with a long streamer dragging behind it that says VISIT DAMIANO'S DREAMWORLD.

And Richard's here. "Do you want a drink?" he asks. I look through the window and suddenly the shadows seem bluer, looser. The endless afternoon is nearly over.

They're all sitting down, waiting, even Isabel. I can hear them from the kitchen: a laugh, then a murmur, like the sound of an audience settling in its seats. Everything is on the table now except the salmon. It's been out of the

71

oven for half an hour, resting and cooling inside its foil. I take a pair of scissors and cut a corner of foil, run the line of the blade along it, then fold it back from the fish. I smear my two hands with butter and ease them under the salmon, then lift. It comes up perfectly, its bright silvery skin intact, and I lay it down again on a bed of fresh dill, on a clean white plate. I wash my hands.

When I bring it in Isabel begins to clap, lightly, her hands level with her eyes so that I can't see them. Edward claps too, his face set in the little ironic smile that is like a tic with him. Richard does not clap. As I put down the heavy dish I see him swallow the saliva that has gathered in his mouth.

"Ooh!" says Susan. "Isn't it beautiful? It seems a shame to eat it."

But we eat it. Its flesh falls from the bones, the color of coral. Its spine shows like a ruined nave. Its eyes have sunk in cooking, and they look inward, filmed like an old man's eyes. Tatters of skin and scale hang from the bones as we eat on, filling and refilling our plates, each mouthful of fish dipped in the sauce, which is not golden at all in this light, but pale as primroses. The salmon's flesh is creamy, with a faint, fresh tang of the sea.

"You can't buy salmon like this," says Richard. "It's a shame Alex didn't stay to eat it."

Isabel puts out her hand and touches Edward's sleeve. "You'll be going up there yourself next week, won't you," she says. "You'll be eating salmon every night."

"Until you're sick of it, like a London apprentice," says Richard, and lifts his glass again, and drinks. He's drunk a lot already. Isabel looks at him, a slight frown stitching itself onto her forehead. Of course, I realize, Isabel's sober. She can't drink because she's feeding the baby. That's why she has that removed, censorious look.

I'm far from sober. As soon as the salmon landed on the table I began to drink. My day of kitchen power was over. Let them stub out cigarettes in the bones of the salmon if they wanted.

The tart is finished and waiting, the cream whipped. The gooseberry fool is chilling. I need do nothing but eat and drink. I drank the first couple of glasses quickly, straight off, on an almost empty stomach, and instantly the room glowed and swam. Now, drinking the third, I remember the wine I had earlier, with Richard. I feel myself raised up as the blue shine of evening strokes the long table, the wrecked and polished skin of the salmon. There are swifts jinking outside the window, and swallows going home to their nests under the barn eaves. I think of owls, fucking the wind. My body goes soft with the thought of it.

Susan has pushed her hair back behind a dark band, so that she looks like a squash player. Her mouth gleams with butter, and her hands cut the food up very small, so it is almost unrecognizable, before she eats it. From time to time she darts a quick look at one face or another. Isabel has stopped eating, though her plate is almost full. She has an unlit cigarette between her fingers, but she seems to have forgotten about it. Richard gets up and moves clumsily past me, on his way to the kitchen for bread. He always wipes his plate with bread. He staggers and puts his hand down hard on my shoulder, for balance.

"Bring in the tart," I say. Susan laughs loudly, and sprays potato through her teeth. Edward turns and scrubs at her with a napkin, like an elder brother, while Isabel leans forward and lights her cigarette from one of the candles, which are suddenly bright, because when I haven't been noticing it, it's gone dark.

Time that I don't notice passes. Richard bangs the tart down on the table in front of me, so hard that I think the crust must have broken. But it hasn't. Usually I can't bear anyone but me to cut into a pie or tart I've made, but tonight I can't be bothered. "Help yourselves. It might as well be eaten," I say, as if the food's nothing. I stare at the apples running rings round the dish. Isabel shakes her head, a tiny shake, and draws on her cigarette. Susan hesitates, looks round again before taking the offered dish and plunging in the knife. She cuts herself a small piece.

"Cut a big piece," says Edward. "You know you want to." Susan giggles, and cuts again. "I'll give you some cream," adds Edward, and lifts the jug.

"Let her do it for herself," says Isabel quietly. Edward glances at her, and puts the jug into Susan's hand.

Richard has filled my glass. I drink off the yellowish wine without bothering to taste it much, though it's good. I take the bottle and fill my empty glass again, right to the top. I am quite drunk, and I want to be much drunker.

"I want to see the owls," I hear myself say suddenly.

"I can show you them if you want. They're nesting in our barn," says Susan.

"Let's all go," says Richard.

"They won't be there now." Isabel stubs out her cigarette. "It's nighttime. They'll be hunting." Then she tenses. "Was that him?" she asks.

"I don't think so," says Susan, spooning cream.

"I'm sure it was." Isabel rises. She's wearing a dress I haven't seen before, a silk dress, long and slim. It's a deep, blackish red, the color of ripe mulberries. Automatically I look down at what I'm wearing. Black trousers, a cream linen shirt. I wonder if I'll ever not feel this pang, so deep it seems to have been put in there by nature.

"I might as well feed him in bed," says Isabel.

"Are you going to bed?" asks Richard. "It's early."

"Not for me. Come in quietly, or you'll wake him up when I've just got him off. Or you could sleep down here, on the sofa. That might be easier." She looks at him and he looks at her, swiveling with that blind, baited look I've seen on him before.

"All right," he says.

chapter *nine*

I STUMBLE on the stairs and bang my shin hard. It seems safest to crawl up the last few stairs and onto the landing, where there's a strip of light under Isabel's door.

"Isabel?"

The door opens and there's Isabel with the baby slung over her shoulder. "What are you doing down there?"

"I've got to sit down, Iz, I feel awful."

"I thought you were drinking a lot."

I sprawl in Isabel's armchair and watch her sit down again, patting the baby's back. The room is too bright, so I shut my eyes.

"I suppose Richard's still boozing."

"He's gone out for a walk with Edward and Susan."

"You should have gone too."

I make a huge effort and open my eyes. "No I shouldn't. Better here."

"I wonder if it's colic. He's all right as long as I do

this, but as soon as I put him down he starts screaming." Isabel stands up and begins to walk the baby up and down, up and down the same strip of floor.

"I can remember doing this with you," she says.

"You can't, can you?"

"I used to put you in the doll's pram and take you for walks. I remember how people used to look in, thinking I had a doll in there, then they'd see it was a real baby. You should have seen their faces. I used to have you all tucked in and parade you up and down the street. Then I'd take you down the hill, holding on tight to the handrail in case the pram ran away with me. It nearly did, lots of times. Everyone used to say I was a proper little mother. I used to think I was the bee's knees. God knows what they thought really."

I watch her walking, her right hand patting Antony's tiny humped back.

"You didn't eat the meal I made," I say suddenly.

"It was wonderful, Neen. Everyone said it was wonderful. But you know I can't eat meals like that."

She looks at me steadily, over the baby's head. I have never heard Isabel admit as much before, though I know it, of course I know it. I've just chosen to pretend that things change and people alter, and Isabel makes it easy for people to pretend. She's always had her breakfast early, she's always going to eat her lunch in the garden, or else she doesn't feel like supper yet. The fact is that

Isabel can't eat round a table with other people. When I look back I can't remember whether she ever could or not. Our mother would leave sandwiches and apples for her under covered plates, and let her go into the larder to fetch what she wanted when she wanted it. I raged because it was so unfair, but for once my mother was immovable.

"Why can't I have Rice Krispies for tea like Isabel?"

"Isabel's different."

I wonder how she's managing. Our mother was always worried that Isabel didn't eat enough, but no one was allowed to say a word to Isabel about food.

"But you're feeding him. Aren't you hungry?"

Isabel points to her bedside table. "Look in the drawer."

"I don't think I can get up."

"Yes you can."

The table, lurches, faraway then close. I snatch at the knob and the drawer slides open.

"There you are," says Isabel, "oatcakes and dried apricots. I eat them all the time, and they're full of iron. So you don't need to worry."

I think of the house filling up with the smells of food all day, and Isabel sitting here, eating an apricot, a quarter of oatcake. Perhaps she did say more about it once. I remember her voice saying something about people's mouths opening and closing, their hands reaching out for food, and all of it unreal and slowed down, as if time was stuck and she was stuck there too. She always hated people who ate too much, except me. She liked me to eat. Yes, now I do remember. There was a time when Isabel used to be able to eat in front of me, as if I were part of herself. But I don't know when it ended.

"I hope the baby won't be like me," says Isabel. "Do you think he will?"

I look at the baby, wheezily sleeping on Isabel's shoulder, limp as a rag. His eyes are so tight shut there is only the thinnest line. "He doesn't look very like you," I say.

"I can't bear to think of what might happen to him," says Isabel, her voice low and intense.

"Nothing's going to happen to him."

"How do you know?" she asks. "How can you tell? Anything could happen. Babies can't tell anybody anything, no matter what happens to them."

"Nothing happened to me, though, did it? And you were only four or five, pushing me all round town."

"He's not like you," says Isabel, so quietly I can hardly hear her. "Look at him. Who do you think he looks like?"

I peer at the baby, but he looks like no one to me. "He's a bit like Dad, isn't he?" I suggest, because someone else has already said it.

"Yes, I suppose so." The tension has gone out of her

voice. "Yes, I suppose he is quite like Dad when you come to look at him."

I'm lying flat on my back on Isabel's bed, without knowing how I got there.

"Don't go to sleep, Neen."

I jump. The tension is back in her voice. "What's the matter?"

"Does the baby look all right to you?"

I prop myself up and inspect the small, shut face. He's the same color as he was earlier, and he seems to be breathing.

"Izzy, of course he's all right. You're just tired. I'll go, then you can get some sleep."

"Don't go, Neen."

"But you've got to rest." And the drink's abandoning me, leaving vast fatigue like mud in an estuary when the tide's gone out. I drag myself off the bed.

"Go and find Edward, then. Tell him I need him."

"But Izzy, he'll have gone to bed."

"He won't. He won't mind."

"Okay, then. Sure you don't want me to stay?"

"It's all right. Get Edward."

I find Edward in the kitchen. We didn't touch the gooseberry fool earlier, but Edward's found it. He sits at the kitchen table with one arm curled round the bowl, digging into it. He raises his spoon in salute.

"Delicious. You really are an excellent cook, Nina."

"Isabel wants you." My tongue feels too big for my mouth, too big for any explanations with Edward. He seems to go at once, or at least, not to be there when I next look. And someone's washed the dishes. I walk back through the dining room, where the table shines, empty. The candles are out, stiff with congealed wax, and the flowers stand in a pool of dropped petals. In the next room, the sitting room, I find Richard asleep on the sofa, facedown, his head hidden in his arms. He's snoring. On the other side of the room there's Susan, sitting on a cushion under the window.

"Oh good," she says, "here you are. Don't worry, he's all right. I've put him in the recovery position."

"What?"

"The recovery position. He'll be perfectly safe."

"What's happened? Did he have an accident?"

"*He was terribly drunk,*" mouths Susan, as if Richard might hear us. "You know there's always a risk of inhaling vomit."

"Good God." I stare at Richard. "You mean you put him lying like that?"

Susan smiles proudly. "They taught us how to lift on the course," she says. "He's a big man, but it wasn't too tricky. Edward couldn't help because he's got a bad back."

"Oh, well. Well done," I say. Susan's eyes shine. She looks like an angel in this light, with her fair hair turned white, standing up round her head and held back by the black band. She brims with questions, her mouth already opening to ask how Isabel is, why Richard's drunk, what I'm going to do with the leftover salmon. But I point at Richard, put my finger on my lips, and back out of the room. It's quite time this evening was over.

I undress in the dark, leaving the curtains open. I wish I was in London now, with orange streetglow coming in through the curtains I'm always meaning to replace with something thicker. I'd like to wake up to a dull day and the swish of tires through rain. This country darkness makes my eyes ache as I try to peer through it. But it's not really dark now. The more I look, the more shadows I see. A soft yellow half-moon is caught in the branches of a tree. Then it breaks free and rises like a bubble of air from a diver. I pull on a navy T-shirt and sit on the bed and watch the sky.

But I must see Isabel. She wanted me to stay, and I didn't. I'm always wanting her to want me, and then when she does I'm out the door. I'd rather listen to her telling me about when I was her baby. I'm her sister, and it was me she wanted, not Edward.

I don't knock. I push Isabel's door open gently, in case she's asleep. And there they are. Edward must have been sitting in the chair beside her bed for a long time. He holds one of Isabel's hands. His left foot is on the cra-

dle rocker, rocking gently, rhythmically, as if he's tread-
ling an old sewing machine. The baby and Isabel are
both asleep. She lies flat, sunk into the bed, her head on
one side. The cradle is facing me, and I can see the
baby's head, his fists up by the sides of his face. Edward
has his back to the door, his head bowed so I think at
first that perhaps he's asleep too. But he's awake. He
hears the door creak. Without letting go of Isabel's
hand, or altering the gentle pressure on the cradle
rocker, he turns his head and looks over his shoulder at
me. He shakes his head, a tiny shake that does not dis-
turb either Isabel or the baby. There's nothing to do but
go away.

I think of the hours Edward spends in Isabel's room,
talking about Alex, making Isabel pour out the oil of her
understanding and advice on him. And giving nothing
back. Why does she do it? Why does she have them
here, Edward and Alex and all the others who come for
supper and stay a week? Exhausting her, draining her,
keeping her from what she really wants to do. I can
never see her alone.

That's how I've always seen it. I suppose everyone
has a story about the people they love, and that's been
mine about Isabel. It's a safe story, well worn and com-
forting. One of those stories children get addicted to,
asking for them again and again and pushing all the
other books aside. Perhaps I tell myself this story so

loudly that I can't hear anything else. Otherwise why would she lie there, sunk in sleep, leaving her baby to Edward? And that look he gave me, as if I'd met his expectation exactly. He knows more about me than I thought.

chapter ten

I FALL INTO SLEEP hungrily, as if it's food, and dreams crowd in. It's because I'm not working. I always dream too much when I'm not working, because all the images I ought to be making lie in wait until I sleep.

I dream of a garden that is Isabel's, but different. The grass in Isabel's garden is burned to the color of a camel by the hot summer, but this grass is soft and green. I'm beside a long border of flowers, backed by a thick yew hedge. The black-green hedge is starred with out-of-season berries, like jam tarts. There are goldenrod and rudbeckia in flower, burning yellow. And there's an overwhelming smell of catnip. I look along and see that the whole border is edged with it. There are small apple trees growing among the flowers, heavy with ripe apples, so heavy that some of the branches have broken and the white, torn wood shows.

Someone's coming. I'm thinking of Isabel, but it isn't Isabel I'm waiting for. I'm alive with excitement. I look down and see I'm wearing a dress I've never seen before.

I feel beautiful and on edge. I'm wearing this dress because I'm going to meet someone, here, now. The name won't come, but it's someone I know well. There are bees all over the border, in the catnip and clinging to the heads of the goldenrod, bending them down with a weight of bee bodies. I start to walk up and down, up and down, feeling my skirt move against my legs.

In the second dream nothing happens. It's a dream about the river, wider and deeper than it is now after weeks of drought. The water's a different color too, like brown glass. I'm standing on the bank looking down. There are tiny pebbles at the bottom, as clear as if they were in my hand, and lodged among them there's a very small plastic doll, a doll's house doll, naked, with wide eyes. The water sways over them and someone says behind me:

Those pebbles are boulders. It's only the depth that makes them look so small.

I try to move back, terrified now that I see how deep this water is, but the same voice says: *Careful. Stay where you are. If you move you'll fall in.*

"Fax for you." Richard hands it to me and I read it eagerly, glad of proof that I've got a life outside this house. I read it again to be sure I've got it right. Yes. The Cruzet

Foundation is going to use me on the Music House project. It means three trips to Romania, two weeks each. They want a different kind of record, sketches as well as photographs. That's why I've got it, because there'll have been a lot of photographers in the running who have more experience than me. I spent a couple of days with a music therapist getting material for a presentation piece, and working out the basis of my proposal. At the time it seemed stupid — a whole two days that I'd never be able to cost into my fee. But you have to be stupid sometimes, to get into the kind of work you really want.

"You look pleased."

"I never thought I'd get it. It's a terrific piece of work."

"I read the fax," says Richard, "but I couldn't make much sense of it. What's the Music House?"

"It's an orphanage in Romania."

"Jesus. You're not going to one of those places, are you?"

"What did you see when I said an orphanage in Romania?"

"I don't know. Newspaper pictures. Kids with shaved heads and big eyes and brain damage. But they're not in the papers anymore, are they? They've had their five minutes."

"That's what this project's about, about it not having

to be like that. The house uses music in everything, so even the kids who can't speak all play in the house band and learn to sing. They choose a piece of music that becomes theirs, like another name. Some of them lost their names, because they were abandoned when they were too young to know them. They each get given an instrument as soon as they come and no one else is allowed to touch it. They'll smash it up but it's always replaced. When they started, most of the instruments were homemade, but now they've been given a lot of stuff and they have a concert every night, after they've eaten. There are two music therapists working out there now, as well as this woman who began it. She still works with the children twelve hours a day. Can you imagine what I'll be able to do, living there for two weeks at a time?"

"I can see why you got the job. You've certainly done the homework," says Richard.

"But it really is unique. No one else has tried anything like it."

"I'm not saying it's not."

I pick up my mug of coffee and drink. I'm longing to look through the fax again, but I'll hold back while Richard's here, since he's clearly not that interested. A green little do-gooder, that's what he makes me feel like. But screw him. He doesn't see what I want. The children separate as droplets, the instruments talking to each other long before the children are able to do so. Groups of children playing together, a single face coming into light then reabsorbed into shadow. I can see splinters of light, splinters of sound. I'll use a camcorder too, then freeze the images and draw from them. I can see myself collaging, drawing across the grain of the prints. In a way, it won't matter what the facilities are like, how rough it is. That's what I want. Rough, immediate, tense work. Like a steel band, but with moments of hush that take your breath away.

"I must fax back. Is that okay?"

"Of course. Use it anytime, and the computer if you like. I was wondering how you were keeping up with your work."

"I've only been here eight days, and I haven't taken a holiday since Christmas."

"Is it only eight days? It seems longer."

"Thanks."

"I didn't mean that," he says. "I didn't mean that, Nina, and you've got me wrong about this Romanian thing too. I admire you."

I flush deeply and turn away, fumbling with the kettle switch. Patter repeats in my head, the patter that I gave Richard, the patter on paper that got me the job. I push in the switch and the kettle hisses dryly.

"I'm very good at boiling up an empty kettle," I tell him.

"Aren't we all."

He is pouched, heavy, shadowed by hangover. He's washed thoroughly in some sharp-smelling soap, and put on a clean white shirt. I recognize the impulse: I've washed my own hair, and it's still wet.

"The sun's getting hot. You could sit outside and dry your hair."

"I thought I'd go in and see Isabel."

"She's talking to Edward." There's no clue to what he thinks or feels. "Let's walk round the garden," he says. "It might clear my head."

The paths keep narrowing, so there is not quite room for two people to walk abreast. I've never noticed this before now, but it's awkward, almost ridiculous. One of us is always having to bob ahead, holding back a branch, or else we're apologizing for bumping into each other.

"Let's sit on this seat," says Richard. It is in the sun, and Isabel has put a terra-cotta pot of golden marjoram beside it. The garden is full of early business, birds slashing at a near-ripe fig, bees fumbling in and out of flowers. We are quite hidden here.

"I think she's getting worse," says Richard.

I say nothing, because I know he isn't talking about the healing of Isabel's wound.

"She hasn't been out in the garden since you came, has she?"

"She must have been." But I think back. Has she?

"I think she tried, the first morning after I was back. Her shoes were wet. But she was back in bed looking awful by the time I woke up. I slept in the armchair."

"She's been in a lot of pain."

"I'm not talking about pain. I don't think she can go outside anymore, do you understand what I mean?"

I understand what he means. It's the same as the food, it all seems so reasonable until you look closely. Isabel doesn't drive, and the buses are awkward. She doesn't visit people. Why trail to London or anywhere else when people can come here? All her city friends can't wait to get away into the country. They come to see her, and they come eagerly, Edward, Alex, and a dozen more. When did she last come to London? I think back. Not since she was pregnant. Not all last summer.

"What about the shopping?" Suddenly, urgently, I want to think of Isabel biking down the track and a couple of miles along the road to the nearest post office, coming back with overpriced mayonnaise and clothes-pegs bouncing in her basket.

"I do it," says Richard. "The only time she's been down that road for months is when she went into hospital. The midwife came here for the antenatal stuff, because she was supposed to be having the baby at home."

"But she was all right in the hospital."

My statement falls into silence. Silence is dangerous.

Two people, the sun falling, getting hotter and hotter on my bare arms and legs. My hair must be nearly dry now. There's the noise of bees, swinging near, veering away again. Farther off, a light chink of metal on metal comes from the barn. The sound of other people at work only makes this bench more private. Richard's face glistens with sweat. He ought to wear a hat. I feel what he feels: the drink, the headache, the hangover, that airy frightened feeling of guilt for things that didn't happen last night — the kind of feeling that makes me want to walk away from myself without making a sound —

We kiss. Not touching much, only our lips. It feels as if there's all the time in the world. He's hot under his shirt, and all the things I forget each time flood back: the tiny movements at first, the kissing deeper and deeper, the thickness of flesh before you touch bone. I thought I'd finished with this greed for the beginnings of things, but it comes again, better than anything I've tried to put in its place. I lean into Richard's heaviness, wanting it to swallow me.

"I've only ever wanted her," says Richard. It's perhaps thirty seconds since the time before we kissed. He's sitting upright, thighs spread, hands clasped, hanging between them.

"I know." But I'm a meticulous noter of tenses. *Up till now,* this means. All I have to think about is what *now* means.

"And you don't love me, you love Isabel," he says, putting his hand over mine.

"I'm not talking about love," I say, and look him full in the face. "But we can have a good fuck and none the wiser."

I watch how his eyes narrow to strips, then widen. His hand tightens on mine. He's looking straight back at me now, and thinking of nothing else. "I'm not like Isabel," I say. "I told you that before. I like food, and I like fucking."

"How many men have you slept with?" asks Richard.

"Nineteen," I say immediately.

"Nineteen? You're sure about that?"

"It could be twenty. Ask me again tomorrow."

"We can't do it here."

"I don't see why not."

"Someone might see."

"I don't think so."

"I see," says Richard. "You like an element of risk."

"There always is one anyway, so why pretend. This is as good as anywhere."

It was as good as anywhere.

"You're not taking off all your clothes, are you?" said Richard.

"Why not? It's still fucking even if I leave my bra on, so why not let's do it properly."

He looks at me and I see a splinter of hesitation swim in his eye, like a minnow.

"You're thinking about those nineteen men," I say. "Don't worry, it's safe."

"I wasn't thinking of that, Nina."

"Then you should have been. That's what things are like. But I haven't got AIDS and I won't get pregnant, so it's safe." I sit down on the seat again, naked. Whatever he does, I'm fine. I could sit here all day soaking up heat and light.

"Women look so different without their clothes on," he says, his voice changing.

"Yes, they do, don't they? How many are you thinking of? Nineteen, is it — or twenty?"

He laughs, sits down beside me, his leg in jeans against my bare leg. The sun burns on us. Richard slides his hand under my breast and watches my nipple stiffen.

"What if Susan came past?"

"She'd think we were about to fuck."

"This bench hasn't got a back," he says. "If I knew you better I could ask you to lie on your stomach across it so I could fuck you from behind. But it's an awkward position."

"That's what you want?"

"It's what I've always wanted."

"Then it's what we'll do."

I have short hair, so it doesn't get in my way, hanging down and trailing on the ground. The position is awkward and the bench would be rough if I hadn't spread Richard's white shirt carefully over it, and used his jeans to make a pillow under my stomach.

"It'll be better if we get down on the ground," says Richard. The grass is short, crisp, and prickling with drought. I get down on hands and knees, then let the weight of my body fall onto my forearms. There is a marigold at eye level, so close I smell its peppery smell. The dry grass under me, the grainy heart of the marigold, the long, still exposure, are all one. I get into position, raising myself, and Richard's finger slides, parting the lips of my wet vulva.

"It looks nice," he says. "You're ready for me, aren't you? I can tell you're ready for me."

He says it with pleasure, with relief, with gratitude, not as some men would say it. The hot sun falls on our wetness and sweat, and a blackbird works away at a grub it's found, less than four feet away. My body stretches, every membrane willing to let him in.

chapter *eleven*

WE'VE ROLLED behind the bench, into the shadow. We're lying there, our skin separating as it cools, when I hear the back door click.

"Put your clothes on," I murmur in Richard's ear. His slack face tightens. We throw on clothes, listening for footsteps, but there aren't any. Then there's a second of standing still, out of breath, Richard looking at me as if there's something more to be said. I smile at him and run my fingers through my hair.

"You look just the same," he says.

"Of course."

He reaches forward, hooks his fingers in the sides of my shorts, and slowly pulls them down. Then he kneels and presses his face into my stomach. I look down on his messed-up, wiry dark hair, but I don't touch it.

"We'll do it again," I say, "but not now. Susan's just come out. I can hear her talking to the baby."

*   *   *

I walk down the little twisting paths on my own, rubbing my fingers on lavender and purple sage. My thighs ache. The paths cross one another, winding between low hedges, so you can walk round the garden many times and never go the same way. Here's a rough patch of gooseberry bushes and blackberries. The gooseberries are finished, but some of the blackberries are ripe, bigger than wild blackberries, fat, shiny, and already black, though it's much too early. The sun's forcing everything. I eat a handful, then sit down on the rough grass so I'm level with the bramble tips feeling their way down to root. I take some things out of my pocket: cigarette papers, a tobacco pouch, a small packet wrapped in silver foil, some matches. I stick the papers together, tear off cardboard from the packet and roll it up, spread tobacco over the paper. I open the foil, light a match, and singe a corner of the brown resin, then crumble it over the tobacco. Then I roll up the joint and twist the end. I wait for a long time before I smoke it. I want to draw those bramble tips as they arch down, nosing their way into earth that is so hard they'll never be able to root. I can hear voices in the distance, but I can't tell whose they are. I close my eyes and sit cross-legged, simmering in a little tent of heat.

I can't get Isabel's doll out of my mind. Yes, I did cut off her eyelashes, thinking they'd grow again. I can still recall the crispy feel of the lashes between the scissor blades. Again and again I wished I'd called my doll Rosina instead of Mandy. One day I began to call her Amelia, but Isabel wasn't having any of that.

"You can't change her name now. How would *you* like it if we all stopped calling you Nina and started calling you Lynn?"

Lynn was my enemy three doors down. I knew Isabel meant what she said, and if I kept on with Amelia she would take away my name as well.

"Let's have a christening," Isabel said.

We'd never been to a christening. Isabel and I used to sit on the wall on Sundays in our bare feet to scorn the tidy churchgoing boys and girls as they came by. Once Isabel took me to a Methodist Sunday school, explaining to the lady there that I was very interested in Jesus and our mummy and daddy wouldn't let me find out about him. This went down well, and the next thing I was coloring a donkey while Isabel won the prize for telling a Bible story in her own words. But the prize was only a packet of Spangles.

"I'm sorry," said Isabel, "our mummy doesn't allow us to eat sweets because of our teeth," and she hauled me off the brown carpet where I was starting on the donkey's tail, which I'd left till last.

"What a load of shit," said Isabel as we skipped off up the hill.

The christening Isabel organized was much better

than Sunday school. We collected all the flowers we could find, the candytuft and marigolds and daisies that grew in our hot, dry garden. Isabel filled a plastic bowl with water, and spread a tablecloth out on the grass. Another tablecloth was going to go round the shoulders of the priest. I could see that Isabel was torn between the two roles of mother and priest, but she solved this by wheeling Rosina and Mandy "to the door of the church," then quickly wrapping herself in her robes while I stood in as mother, clutching the dolls. Isabel muttered words I couldn't hear properly, and sprinkled flowers on the dolls' upturned faces. Then she seized Rosina and plunged her into the water. A second later Rosina bounced up to the surface, water rolling off her plastic skin.

"Right, she's done," said Isabel in her normal voice, then she took Mandy. Mandy went down as Rosina had done, but unlike Rosina she stayed there, bubbles of air streaming up from her soused curls.

"Oh dear," said Isabel, "I'm afraid she's stuck. Don't worry, mother, I'll pull her out." But I saw her hands tensed, pushing Mandy down. "She doesn't want to come up, I'm afraid," said Isabel.

"Get her up! Get her up!" I screamed.

Isabel grunted, pushing and pulling at the same time. Suddenly Mandy shot out of the bowl on a wave of water onto the parched grass and lay there still, facedown and sodden. Isabel rushed to her and knelt down, her table-cloth robe hiding Mandy from my sight. I stood rooted. Slowly, Isabel turned. Her face was wet with real tears.

"I'm sorry, mother, I'm so sorry. Your little baby has drowned."

I shut my eyes so as not to see what Isabel was holding, and screamed and screamed. My screams rang in my head, red as the sun through my closed eyelids. As long as I kept screaming nothing else could happen. I heard a sash window bang up, then Isabel grabbed my shoulders, shaking me, shouting, "She's all right! Look, she's sitting up! It's a miracle!"

But I could not stop screaming, though I opened my eyes and saw Mandy sitting rigidly on the grass, her eyes staring blindly ahead of her. Our mother came out of the back door, wiping clay from her hands. Isabel rushed to her.

"Nina's crying because Mandy fell in the water and she thinks she's dead. I keep telling her she isn't, but she won't listen."

My mother knelt on the grass beside me and put one arm round me, and I stopped screaming. "Isabel, give Mandy to me."

My mother took the doll, turned her over, and patted her back. "That's to get the water out of Mandy's lungs. Now I'm going to turn her over and give her the kiss of life. Watch."

My mother put her lips over Mandy's face. Slowly, gently, she breathed out into Mandy's mouth. She turned aside, took another breath, and breathed into Mandy again. After a while she stopped and said, "There. It's working. Her color's coming back. She just had a shock, Nina. She wasn't really drowned."

I took Mandy from my mother. She felt soft again, and warm from my mother's skin. Her eyes looked at me, smiling.

"She's all right now," said my mother. "Pour the rest of that water away, Isabel."

Isabel poured away the water, and it sparkled on the dry earth, then sank in. I watched her, rocking Mandy, and my mother went back into the house.

How long was that after Colin died? Two months, maybe.

I smoke some of the joint, not much. The baby's crying, and I hear the whine of a car coming up the track in low gear and then the crunch of its tires. I see bits of Richard's body in bright flashback, disconnected, and myself too, my hands pulling off my clothes, then flexing against the ground. I feel like someone who is running faster and faster but still finding breath.

chapter *twelve*

MARGERY WILKINSON'S sitting in the kitchen, holding the baby while Susan makes a pot of coffee. Her eyes rest on me, bright and curious, and I wonder what Susan's been telling her. She holds the baby expertly, even I can see that. She's wrapped his cotton shawl differently, tight, like a swaddling shawl. You'd think he'd be too hot, but he looks much more comfortable with her than he does with any of us. He's wide awake, his big navy eyes scanning her face.

"Wide awake and not crying," I say. "There's a miracle."

"It's just a knack," Margery says. "I've had four, don't forget."

You wouldn't guess it to look at her. Like Susan, she's blond, but in Margery's case it's an expensive blondness that has to be renewed every three weeks or so. She always wears a lot of gold jewelry; once she told Isabel she was collecting gold. Isabel's been half promised a sight of the collection, though of course you have to be careful, with insurance premiums the way they are these days. Margery is a carefully dieted woman too, who still looks good in her jeans and white shirt.

"I haven't seen your sister," she says to me, a faint accusation in her voice. "She's gone to sleep, Susan says."

"She's supposed to rest a lot."

"Apparently she's been playing cards with someone called Edward half the morning. I don't call that resting."

"Oh good," I say, "she must have been feeling better."

"You had quite a party here last night, so Susan was telling me. I didn't realize you were such a keen cook, Nina. You'll have to give me some new ideas. I get sick of my own cooking, don't you? But of course it's different if you haven't got a family. I've the Young Farmers barbecue next week, and my boys'll play war if it's not better than last year's. Of course, Susan'll help me out, but you wouldn't believe the amount they eat. This baby's hungry — look at him."

The baby is mouthing her shirt, making mewing sounds. "He wants his bottle," says Margery, staring hard at Susan.

"Mum, he's breast-fed." Her tone makes it clear they've had all this before.

"Oh, I know it's all the fashion these days. But I can tell you, Susan, when you've got three under four the way I had, you'll be glad of bottles. At least you can see what they're getting. I should have taken out shares in Ostermilk."

"He's doing fine. The health service visitor weighed him and he's put on four ounces."

"You can weigh him all you like, but he looks hungry to me, and I know a hungry baby when I see one." Her rings flash as she shifts the baby to her other arm.

"Give him your finger to suck, Mum, that'll keep him quiet."

"What do *you* think, Nina? Doesn't it seem daft to you, your sister breast-feeding when she's had a hysterectomy? How is she going to get her strength back?"

"It's what she wants to do."

"She doesn't know *what* she wants. How can she? You don't know if you're coming or going after a first baby. And a major operation on top of it, it's not surprising she's in the state she is."

In the state she is. What's Susan been saying? "And it's not just the physical side of things. You're going to have to watch out for this postnatal depression." She watches me as I move round the kitchen. "It's nice she's got a sister to come down. I only ever had Geoffrey's mother, and that was a very mixed blessing, I can tell you. There are some people you want near you when you're not quite yourself, and she wasn't one of them. Who is this Edward, then?"

"Oh, he's an old friend of Isabel's. You must have met him before, he's always coming down."

"I *see*."

I catch Susan's eye over her mother's head and Susan winks, a little fleeting wink that is much more sophisticated than anything I've ever heard her say.

"And here's Richard," says Margery, turning, crossing her legs, "back from foreign parts. Where was it this time?"

"Korea." He slides easily into a chair by Margery's.

"Do you want coffee, Richard?" I ask, unhooking more mugs.

"Yes, why not?"

"That plane must have been over us ten times yesterday if it came over once. Doesn't it drive you mad?" asks Margery, stirring sweetener into black coffee. "I wonder it stays in the air, it's so slow."

"I heard they were going to close down," says Susan.

"What, Damiano's Dreamworld? Never. It's been going since you were six. We took you for your birthday, the month it opened, don't you remember?"

"I wonder if anyone's done a survey," says Richard, "into the effectiveness of aerial advertising?"

"Don't suggest it," says Margery. "Now we've got two so-called universities down the road instead of one, half the world's surveying the other half. I'm only grateful Susan went into something sensible. The world's her oyster, isn't it, Susan?"

"Yes," says Susan.

"I'd love to go to Damiano's Dreamworld," I say.

"We could all go, when Isabel's better," Richard says. "And we'll make a point of telling them we only came because of the plane."

"It would certainly do Isabel good to get out more," says Margery, with more meaning in her voice than I like. "Richard, *you* ought to have a word with her. This baby's starving. Look at him, gnawing my arm with his little gums. And Susan's not thought to get so much as a tin of milk in the house, let alone a bottle."

"Isabel doesn't want him to have any," says Richard.

"Well, she isn't going to know, is she, if Susan gives him a little bottle when he's hungry?" Margery's eyes gleam. "You could always tell her later on, when she's better."

I bend down and put my awkward hands round the baby. "I'll take him." I lift him carefully away from Margery, but not too carefully. I've noticed how firmly Margery grasps him, and how he seems to like it. I tuck him into the crook of my arm and begin to walk him up and down. He doesn't cry. His eyes stare at me without quite seeming to see me, then they droop and close fast over his eyes. "There," I say, "he's asleep. He must have been tired." I look up and see Richard watching me, his eyes moving over my body as if matching it against some pattern in his head. I look back, briefly. I'm still wearing the shorts he pulled down. I cover my thoughts so that Margery won't see them with her round, bright eyes.

"You ought to put him down now he's off," says Susan. "We don't want him to get used to being held all the time, do we?"

"God forbid," says Richard. "He'll have a terrible time when he grows up. Bring him through, Nina, and I'll open the doors for you."

"He could go in my room," says Susan. "Then you won't wake Isabel."

"Okay." Richard holds the kitchen door open, and I pass under his arm holding the baby. Just as I do so, I realize that it's his baby I'm carrying. Richard's child. I've always thought of the baby as Isabel's alone. I glance back, toward him, but I catch Margery looking at me, taking in the three of us, Richard, the baby, me. She knows nothing. She's just letting her instincts play on us and seeing what they come up with. She probably doesn't even know she's doing it. It's people like Margery you have to look out for.

Richard and I walk carefully as far as the stairs, as if Margery's still with us.

"I can manage Susan's door fine. You go back now."

"You won't know how to turn on the baby alarm."

He comes up behind me. Susan's room is beyond the bathroom, badly planned so that a turn of corridor cuts off about a quarter of its space. It has a single pine bed, a chest with a TV on it, a table and chair looking over the garden. Sometimes the baby sleeps in here so Isabel isn't disturbed. There's a carrycot on the floor, and his changing things on a trolley with a mobile of zoo animals hanging over it. All the furniture is new and quite unlike anything in the rest of the house. There's a teddy bear on the bed, and a pile of magazines. I lay the baby on his side, and loosen the shawl. He's gathered into himself, fast asleep, and he doesn't move as I settle him. Then I straighten up.

"There. We'd better get back." Richard stretches out a hand, but I step back.

"Not in the house."

"I just wanted to touch you."

"I'm going back to the kitchen now. When Margery's gone I'll be out under the cherry tree behind the compost heap. It's nice there."

His face looks hard, heavy and tired. He glances down at the baby, then back at me. "Do you really want to?"

"Of course."

Back in the kitchen Margery and Susan are pouring themselves second mugs of coffee.

"He's gone down."

"Good," says Susan. "He ought to sleep till lunch-time now."

"Your sister'll get a nice rest," adds Margery, picking up her coffee, drinking it, looking at me. "I must say, Nina, you're looking *very* well, I don't think I've ever seen you looking so well. Though I wouldn't have thought of you as a shorts person."

"They're easy in this weather," I say, "and it doesn't matter what you wear down here, does it?" I notice that she's unable to stop herself glancing down at her crisp white shirt. Her mouth moves slightly, as if she'd like to tell me how much it costs and how tricky it is to iron. But instead she recrosses her legs and says, "I suppose you *are* on a sort of holiday."

The joint has made me hungry, and there are almond slices in the cake tin above Margery's head, if Edward hasn't found them. I reach up, leaning over her, and bring down the tin. It's light, too light. I open it and there is only one slice left, with the glacéed cherry picked out of it.

"I was going to offer you some cake," I say, "but there's nothing left except this bit. Oh dear, it's gone stale. Never mind, I'll finish it off." The cake is delicious, synthetically moist and sweet. I eat it quickly and put the tin in the sink.

"Oh well, time for work."

"Are you going to do some drawings, Nina?" asks Susan.

"I'd love to see them," says Margery. "Susan's been telling me about all this drawing. I thought you were a photographer, but now it turns out you're an artist as well."

"I'm going to draw in the garden," I say.

"Does being watched put you off?" asks Susan, her face turning a slightly deeper pink.

"It does rather." I break a banana off a bunch and smile at Margery.

"Goodbye. I don't expect I'll still be here next time you come."

"You never know," says Margery. I'm sure it's just one of the things she says all the time, but it sounds as if she means to sit there, on and on, watching what we do, gathering evidence.

Richard is already under the tree. "Nina —"

"It's not going to be any good if you talk," I say.

The talking rises in his eyes, and dies down. With its fermenting smell of compost, its shade and soft earth, the cherry tree is a better place than the bench.

"But I need to pee first," I say.

"You could go behind the tree. I shan't watch."

"Or here."

"Can you do that? I'd be too tense in front of you." He watches me, his hands stopped in undoing his belt. Suddenly he shivers. "Jesus, Nina. You should be careful."

"I've already told you I'm careful."

"No, I mean, some blokes would think they could do anything."

"But you don't think that."

"I don't know what to think."

"I don't know what 'anything' means."

"I could show you."

"You could show me."

The earth under the cherry tree is soft and warm where layers of grass cuttings have been thrown. I'm on my face, like a swimmer bruised from a slow crawl up pebbles against the drag of the sea. I roll over and look straight up at the sky, cut into chinks by wide-ribbed cherry leaves. The sky is white, the cherry leaves black. It's nearly noon, the hour when ghosts walk, and this hot summer I can see why. When I go down the track at noon I feel as if I'm dwindling, without a shadow, my head forced into my shoulders by the sun. That's how a ghost knows it's a ghost, because it makes no mark on the earth where it walks.

Richard's eyes are shut. His hands lie at his sides, unclenched, palms upward. His chest moves regularly with his breathing, but his mouth is closed and I don't think he's asleep. He looks content, fucked out. I like his silence.

I can remember Colin's funeral. His coffin was so small that my father carried it down the aisle of the white church as if it was a baby. My mother had told me it wouldn't really be Colin in the box, just his body, which he didn't need anymore. I nodded, but I didn't know what she meant. After my bath that night, the night before the funeral, I curled up in my towel behind the bathroom door, smelling my own smell, nuzzling the warmth of my legs and arms. Isabel was sitting on the lavatory by the bath, straining to go. I watched her face flush, then turn pale. I tried to think of me and Isabel without bodies, but I couldn't.

I don't know where the church was, but I know it wasn't in St. Ives. There were a lot of people there, but no other children, and when my father walked down toward the door with the coffin there was a murmuring noise, like leaves, as people turned their heads toward him and then away. My mother was there too, at his side, her head down, wearing a dress I'd never seen before. That was important, because I knew the feel and smell of all her dresses. The green velvet with the velvet rose on the hip was my favorite, but she only wore it on special occasions. She should have been wearing it now, instead of that crinkly black stuff that smelled of shops. After we all came in I was lifted onto a seat with other people who must have been friends, but I can't remember who they were.

I was there, but Isabel wasn't; it's the only important memory from my childhood where she doesn't feature. She was in bed. For weeks after Colin's death Isabel had terrible stomach pains, so bad that sometimes she couldn't breathe. My mother would make little meals for her on a tray. Once she had two delicate lamb cutlets with a pool of mint sauce on the side. It was grown-up, expensive food, but she wasted it. I saw the tray on the kitchen table, with white lamb fat sticking the chops to the plate. I think that was the beginning of Isabel's not eating with us.

Richard's fallen asleep now. He looks older, his chin sinking into the flesh under it. We talked a bit, not much. He asked how old I was, he knew I was younger than Isabel but he couldn't remember how much. I told him I was twenty-nine.

"And I'm forty-six," he said. "Well into the era of dental floss and bleeding from orifices." He smiled, and I saw lots of fillings in his back teeth.

A leaf detaches itself from the tree, spins down, and falls on him. I wait for another. Drought's hitting the trees now, after burning grass and bushes brown. The trees survive by seeming to die: they're shedding their leaves in self-protection, drawing all their sap back to the heart. It's like an early autumn, but a strange autumn with the sun blazing on a fall of crisp brown leaves.

I get up very quietly. I've got no shadow here either, because we're already in shade, so nothing passes over his face to wake him. I pick up my clothes and shake them out, then put them on. Already, with the fallen leaves on his chest, Richard looks as if he's been lying there a long time. It doesn't matter if anyone else finds him here lying naked on the ground, alone. People do strange things when it's as hot as this.

chapter *thirteen*

"I FEEL WONDERFUL." Isabel's up, dressed, sitting on the bed fastening her sandal. She's wearing a very pale green dress, and she's brushed her hair up on top of her head and fixed it with a comb. She looks cool and happy. "I slept all night, then I woke up early and played piquet with Edward, and I've been asleep for another two hours at least. I feel like a different person."

"The baby's asleep in Susan's room."

"I thought I might take him out after lunch." Isabel looks up at me with her long, clear look. She has the blue eyes that should belong to a blond, but set in her golden face they look strange, unsettling, as if their clarity is part of a deception.

"But you haven't got a pram."

"I'll take him in the sling, like Susan does. Edward's going to come with me."

"Where will you go?"

"Nowhere much. Round the garden, maybe down the track a bit." Her eyes widen. Her face is so calm that it would be impossible to guess how frightened she is, unless you knew her. She feels better and she's going to test herself, as she must have done the other morning when she came back with her shoes soaked. I hope Edward knows what's going on.

"Are you sure you're up to it?" I ask casually, as if the only thing that worries me is the operation she's had.

"I'm supposed to walk. I was thinking back, and you won't believe it, Neen, you know what I'm like about the garden, but I realized I hadn't been outside since he was born."

Isabel is a very good actor. She mimics perfectly the surprise anyone might feel at suddenly realizing she's been housebound for days.

"You've had a major operation," I say. "It's not surprising."

She looks at me gratefully. "I know. I keep forgetting. I keep thinking I ought to be doing things."

"You mustn't push yourself." I want Isabel to be well and happy, free to go where she wants. And I want to keep Isabel out of the garden, which is becoming my territory.

"I think I must," she says quietly. Her hands are flat on the bed at her sides, ready to push herself up. She's still moving cautiously, afraid to wake pain.

"The baby," I say suddenly. "I've only just realized. I knew he reminded me of someone."

"Who?"

"He looks like Colin."

"Colin?" Isabel's face goes quite still, then her mouth falls open, so that for a second she looks not beautiful at all. For a moment I'm terribly afraid that she's going to say, *Who is Colin?* She licks her lips. "Colin. Do you think so?"

"It's been nagging at me ever since I first saw him. I thought he looked like Dad, and of course he does, but then Colin looked like Dad as well. Everyone said so."

"I don't remember what Colin looked like," says Isabel.

"You must. You were older than me, and I remember him."

"No. I've never been able to. If I shut my eyes and try to see his face, all I see is a sort of . . ." She pauses, shuts her eyes. "Disk."

"I can remember him quite well." I frown, doubting myself now. "At least, I think I can. He was big, and fair. But I suppose he might have looked big to me because I was little too. His head was wobbly."

"Don't let's talk about it, Neen."

"I'm sorry, Isabel, I didn't mean —"

"You forget," she says sharply, angrily, "I've got a baby myself now. Of course I'm going to worry about cot-death. I would anyway, let alone after what happened to Colin. Do you think I haven't thought it might happen to him? I think about it every single night when I put him down."

"I didn't mean it like that." A feeling stirs in me, like something coming to life, but I don't know if I can explain it to Isabel. "It's not a sad thing. He's not going to die like Colin, I know he isn't. It's the thought that Colin hasn't really gone, not completely. You know what it was like, it seemed as if he'd just disappeared. You remember how we looked in his room and the bed was gone, and everything. And Mum never being happy again, it all seemed completely pointless." It's only at that moment, as I say those words, that I admit to myself that my mother never was happy again after Colin's death. She worked, she looked after us, she smiled, she had friends, but her happiness had gone. I never wanted to believe it. I would sit in her lap more than I'd ever done, playing with a long necklace of amber that she had, warming the beads in my hand, singing and humming like a little girl who was happy.

"It was pointless," says Isabel. "I don't see why you want to talk about it." Her sureness stamps down on the stirring thing that I can't quite put into words. Perhaps all I remember is a disk, too. But I don't think so. I don't easily forget anything I've seen, once I've really looked at it. I remember a baby's face, turned sideways in a bed.

I'd tiptoed in alone, feeling guilty, because Isabel

never played with the baby and I always wanted to be the same as Isabel. But I also wanted to see him. He was awake, but not crying, peeping through the bars at some dancing light on the opposite wall. There was so much light when we were growing up, coming up off the sea, so that even on a gray day my eyes stung with it. The baby moved his head, hearing me come in, and then a big gummy smile spread across his face. I peered in at him through the bars. His arms and legs waved like weed in a rock pool. He could turn his head but he couldn't roll over. There was a special smell all round his room, a baby smell. He dabbed at a string of spools my mother had hung across the bed, but his fist went wide. Both his legs kicked in the air, and he turned to me and smiled again. His head was lying on a muslin cloth that my mother would put over her shoulder. His hair stuck up in sweaty feathers. I stood there for quite a long time, then I went away.

Edward opens the door without knocking. "He's woken up, Isabel. Susan's changing him, then if you feed him we can go straight out." He's got the sling dangling from one hand.

"All right, I'll just —" says Isabel, and she hurries out of the room.

"She looks awful," says Edward, staring after her. "What's happened? She was fine when she woke up." He drops the sling on the bed, a bright coil of nursery stripes. Then he turns to me with an edge of real dislike in his voice. "What have you been saying to her?"

"Nothing."

"You don't think I notice anything, do you, Nina?"

"You come across as fairly self-absorbed, yes."

"Not where Isabel's concerned."

"Jesus, Edward, what is this thing about Isabel? Anybody would think you were in love with her. If they didn't know you."

"I do love Isabel, as it happens. Isn't it interesting, Nina — you think you're so liberated, but really all you see when you look at me is 'Isabel's gay friend.' You can't look beyond that."

"It's not that I can't. It's that I'm not interested enough to do so."

"You're not all that interested in Isabel, either, are you? I think you're a shit, Nina, but since she doesn't see through you I'll keep my thoughts to myself."

I'm bad at dealing with people who don't like me. A bit of me wants them to, even though I know it's not going to happen, and I don't like them at all myself. And I've always found it unbearable to think of affection flowing toward Isabel, and a blank face turned to me. But I fight it now. I can be hard and cold.

"You do that," I say. "Isabel and I are sisters. We share a past that you don't know anything about and can't possibly understand."

"I hope that's all you share," says Edward.

The words gleam, so double-edged they cut wherever they touch.

I watch them from Isabel's window, walking down the paths. The sling is round Edward, because the pull of it was uncomfortable for her. They look small and happy, walking slowly to and fro across the lawn, bending to look at things that are too small for me to see, disappearing down paths, between shrubs, then reappearing. Once, I hear Isabel laugh. Beyond the wall the meadows are bleached, with a diagonal green scar running across one of them where there must be water just under the ground. I move to the side of the window, where I can see and not be seen, and just then Isabel and Edward come out of the trees and walk toward the house. Edward stops and hitches at the sling, trying to adjust it, but it fastens at the back. Isabel goes behind him and fiddles with the clip while he bends at the knees to make it easier for her. When she's made the adjustment they both turn to look down the garden, with their backs to me, shading their eyes against the glare of the midday sun. On the back of Isabel's pale green dress, between her shoulder blades, there is a dark patch of sweat.

chapter *fourteen*

THE SEA WAS there all the time. I would wake in the
night and listen to the sea until it took me back into
sleep. When we were older Isabel and I slept in the attic
that ran the length of our narrow terraced house, our
beds under each of the dormer windows. We looked out
over Porthmeor Beach, over the Island, at the shining
trail left on the sea by fishing boats heading west from
the harbor. On winter nights storms punched the wall
by my ear and our house shuddered before the wind. If
the storm came by day Isabel and I would go out in it, in
our yellow oilskins and hats, to watch the sea boil and
the spray explode at the base of the cliffs.

The sea got into everything. Our leather school sandals were white with salt before we'd had them a week.
Later they would rot at the seams, long before we'd
grown out of them. There was sand in the carpets, sand
in the grass. Every year my mother would slap paint on
every window frame she could reach, so that the sea
would not eat down to the wood. Wind and salt scoured

off paint and covered the windows with spray. Our hair was sticky, whipped into tangles until we couldn't get a comb through it. Each summer one streak bleached white over my forehead. In winter there were thick white mists that clung to us like cobwebs, and the noise of a foghorn lowing, then the air would begin to move again, and black humps of rock would slide out of the silence. When the fog was heavy I kept my mouth shut, frightened that it would get into my throat and choke me. But Isabel danced ahead, just out of sight, daring the fog to swallow her up. Our father had a rhyme for Isabel:

> *Isabel, Isabel, met a bear.*
> *Isabel, Isabel, didn't care . . .*

I thought he'd made it up for her, and was surprised to find it in a book years later, with someone else's name under it.

He was often away. He was a poet, but not the poet he wanted to be. He was a very good critic, and he couldn't stop being one when he looked at his own work. I still try to read his poems sometimes. You can find his collections in secondhand bookshops, and they don't cost very much. There's something terrible about the way titles of books fade. He wrote poems about us, but he didn't see us very much. He had to spend a lot of time in London, where he did his reviewing and critical articles. St. Ives was my mother's place, and if he wasn't there too often, I suppose he could avoid seeing how much better she was as a potter than he was as a poet. Although I don't think he was the sort of man who could easily avoid seeing things.

He was a handsome man, our father, and five years younger than my mother. He was fair, with the same eyes as Isabel, the same golden skin, which was creased by the time I knew him. By some reckonings my mother was lucky to get him. He drew people round him, because he was funny, because he had a way of making you feel that you were something new and delightful he'd just discovered, and above all because there was something lost and pained in him which people felt without knowing quite what it was. He seemed to need you. My mother didn't seem to need anybody much. Only after Colin died I heard her cry out, behind a door, and I thought she'd called my name. I slid the door open. It was dark because the curtains were pulled over the window, but I could see her. She was lying on her face, clutching the pillow. Her head thumped from side to side. My father was sitting on the bed, smoking a cigarette, and he saw me because the light changed as I opened the door. My mother didn't notice. He just looked up and shook his head slightly, and I went out again.

A bit later she went away for a while. My father

looked after us on his own, the only time I can remember his doing that. We loved every minute of it. A weight had gone out of the house, and though Isabel still had stomach pains and didn't eat much, she seemed much happier once our mother had gone. He didn't cook at all. In the mornings we had cornflakes, at lunchtime we had money for fish and chips, at night he took us out. Things must have been going quite well then. There seemed to be money for going out and for real shopping. Sometimes we just had what we couldn't do without, fetched each day from the corner shop by me and Isabel.

We went out late, because my father hated eating early. We had steak and chips, or spaghetti. Isabel ate too. I watched her out of the corner of my eye the first night, when the waitress put the plate of steaming sauce and wriggly spaghetti down in front of her. But she ate it, wrapping up the pasta on her fork expertly, in a way I couldn't manage. I forgot to eat my own food, stopped in my tracks by Isabel's cleverness.

The next night the waitress leaned over me and whispered to us, "I've got something you'll like." She brought two plates from behind her back. On each there was a chocolate teddy bear, gleaming brown. Their skin had a mist of cold on it.

"It's ice cream inside," said the waitress, and watched us, smiling. I picked up my spoon but it was too beautiful to eat.

"Go on. It'll only melt."

I tapped the chocolate as if it was a boiled egg. Immediately tiny cracks sprayed over the chocolate, showing the white ice cream underneath. I looked at Isabel to see what she was doing, but she hadn't touched hers. Isabel was always able to wait for things. This was different, though. Her hands had dropped to her lap, and her face was closed. She wasn't going to eat it.

"Don't you like it?" the waitress asked Isabel. Her voice was cross with disappointment.

"I'd rather have fruit salad," said Isabel in a tiny thread of a voice. Saying nothing, the waitress swept up the plate with the chocolate teddy bear on it and bounced out. I dug deep into mine and began to eat fast, hardly tasting it, hoping I'd have finished it by the time the waitress got back.

Isabel's salad looked sour. Our father gave the waitress one of his big, soft smiles. "You're very good," he said, "but I don't think she feels much like eating at the moment. She's still upset."

The waitress's face went weak, and she nodded, looking at Isabel in a quite different way. "Of course, the little one's too young to feel it the same," she said. I ate on, my face burning, the chocolate teddy bear slipping round the plate as I chased it with my spoon.

Once the waitress had gone our father hummed to himself, quietly,

Isabel, Isabel, met a bear.
Isabel, Isabel, didn't care . . .

I loved his face when it crinkled up with laughing, or with trying not to laugh. He seemed to find us funny most of the time, even when we weren't trying to be. Soon after this, he told me he was thinking of starting a pudding club, and I could be in it if I liked. The only rule was that members had to discover at least four new puddings a year. I didn't see how I was going to discover any puddings, as I had no money of my own, but he told me that one day he would take me to London and we'd go to a place where they did nothing but puddings. When I was big and had learned to read he would buy me a book of puddings and I could learn to cook them.

"It's no good relying on your mother and Isabel. They're fruit salads, the pair of them."

Of course, my father had a woman in London, and she wasn't a fruit salad. I met her later on; she was called Amy Ludgate. He married her for a year after my mother's death, before he died too. My mother had expected to die, because she'd had breast cancer for two years, but my father hadn't. He went out almost between one step and the next, on his way back from the launch of someone else's new collection. It was an aneurysm, a weakness no one had known about. He hadn't made a will and there wasn't any money, but

Amy offered us his manuscripts. She was sure they'd be worth a lot one day. Besides, we were his daughters, and she thought we had a right to them, whatever the law said. She was generous, Amy. She could love things and not want to own them. She never stopped fighting the battles against neglect that my father would not fight for himself. But we knew no one was ever going to care for his poetry as much as she did, so we said she should keep the manuscripts, and she has them still. I had a letter from her not long ago saying she'd made her will, and naming the university library she had chosen to have his papers. I only hope they're willing to take them.

He'd been with Amy before Colin was born. Colin was a fluke, not an attempt at reconciliation. I found out later that my parents hadn't slept together for two years before he was born. But my father was down from London for a few days and they sat for a long time over a meal after we went to bed, drinking rich red wine that my father had brought back from France. And so they stumbled into bed, and later there was Colin. No, not stumbled. They weren't that drunk, my mother said. They still knew what they were doing. It was very important to her to be accurate about things like that, and not to give us false ideas about what had happened between them. I suppose it was a good thing, but it could feel a bit bleak. Colin was born, and then he died, and his death brought them closer than his life had done, for a while.

My father wrote a poem that was read at Colin's funeral. I didn't understand a word of it, and I couldn't work out why he was suddenly standing up at the front and reading it, when I knew this wasn't a poetry reading. One odd thing followed another, like strange fish you have to separate from the catch and throw back.

I can still taste that chocolate teddy bear. Cold, sweet, tender, the splintered chocolate giving way to smoothness. In fact I can taste it better now than I could then as I rushed to please the waitress. I see us all: Isabel poking at a segment of tinned grapefruit, with her face in shadow as her long hair slipped forward; my father smoking and chatting with the waitress over our heads; and me kicking the chair legs and waiting for someone to admire my nice clean plate.

When both your parents are dead great slabs of the past drop away like eroded cliffs. I want my past back. I need it now, to ask it the questions I never realized I needed to ask. But there's nothing. Silence, and the shining of the sea where once there was land. I have Isabel's stories. She's made a story of the past which I used to accept without question. She's so persuasive that it doesn't seem like persuasion, but like the truth. Edward is persuaded. There they are, walking again side by side, but even more slowly now, as if the heat of the sun is pressing them down. No. It's not that. Something's wrong. She isn't walking right. I lean forward and push up the window, and at the same moment Edward grabs Isabel's arm, but she buckles away from him, very slowly, her body folding up and dropping to the grass. He kneels. The baby's in the way, the sling hampers him. He can't get at her, can't lift her and turn her over. He turns, looking for help, and sees me watching.

chapter *fifteen*

ISABEL SHOULD NEVER have gone outside. The sun at midday is hotter than it's been for two hundred years. Ladybirds swarm, clay-puddled dew ponds crack in the heat, empty. The Downs are yellow-brown, like the flanks of lions. At midday the emptiness of the sky and the pounding of the sun are frightening. But then evening comes, and the light liquefies to yellow, and Isabel's absent, knocked out.

It's evening now. Past nine, getting dark, and I'm in the garden. I'm watering Isabel's apple trees bucket by bucket, because it's forbidden to use a hose. I'm thinking of Isabel and sickness. The afternoon's been full of it, the doctor coming, the midwife calling in to check up, the health visitor advising Isabel on feeding. Isabel says she wants to stop breast-feeding the baby now. It's making her ill. The health visitor says she's doing so well, she mustn't give up. "Mustn't?" says Isabel, and she shuts her eyes, turning her silky brown shoulder on everyone. Later she tells Richard to drive into town and buy bottles and tinned milk. Everything turns on Isabel. And hasn't it always, since she lay in bed, in pain, while our brother was buried.

I am sick of it all. Milk and blood and babies. I lug another bucket down the path, the dark water shivering inside it. Water slops over my bare feet and raises scent from the dust. These trees should never have been planted in a drought. I heft the bucket and walk on, all my skin prickling with attention. I'm waiting. I leave the full bucket standing by the trees and wander on through the gloom, down to the raspberry canes. There are big moths flying. When they land patches of white show up on their wings so they look like jigsaws. Daytime life closes down, and night life begins with its own excitement. I wish I were in the city now, where day and night brush each other for hours. I wish I were in a taxi, hurling round the corners of parks as they turn from blue to black with dusk.

There's a tall, thick double row of canes. Some have finished fruiting, others are still in season. I feel for berries in the dark and find them, their ripe seeds melting on my tongue. I hear feet on the path behind me, but I keep on picking, prolonging that moment of not looking round.

It's gone much darker. Most of the garden has

been gulped down into shadow, but white flowers glow across it.

"Give me one," Richard asks.

I pick off a berry and hold it to his lips. He's half opened his mouth, ready. "I could have given you anything," I say. "What if that was deadly nightshade?"

"You wouldn't do that."

"What's going on?"

"Nothing. Isabel's asleep. They've moved the baby into the cot because the health visitor thought he'd sleep better."

I move away, down the row.

"Come here."

"I'm picking raspberries for tomorrow."

"What are you wearing? I can't see."

"My blue dress. The short one."

"I'll help you." He pushes after me down the hollow grassy passage between the raspberry canes. I want to run, but I make myself keep still, feeling under the leaves for the slight furriness of the fruit. The berries are warmer than the leaves. He touches my arm, but I twist and move on.

"Nina."

"Yes."

He's behind me, his hands running up my thighs under my dress. I lean back against him, opening my legs, aching.

"Do you want another?"

He opens his mouth and I push in raspberries. His hand is between my thighs, feeling for the opening of my vagina. He slides in a finger, two fingers. I turn my cheek against his arm. He's changed from a white to a denim shirt, and I know why. The glint of a white shirt carries a long way through the dusk.

"You want it."

"You know I do."

"That's what you came here for."

"Of course it is."

He sighs, and we slide down. It's damp here, between the canes, and dark. He's kicking off his jeans, and I pull up my dress.

"Not like that. Take all your clothes off like you did last time."

It's a loose, short dress and it comes off easily. I roll it into a ball and toss it out of the way.

"That's better."

We lie lengthways between the canes, hot, slippery, naked.

"Say what you said before."

"What?"

"Say we can always have a good fuck."

"I don't need to. You know it already."

"But say it."

"We can always fuck."

"Always."

"When we want."

"Now."

He lies underneath me. I ease myself down onto him slowly, and we start to move. I'm on an endless staircase, going down, going nowhere.

I fall asleep for a minute afterward, a brief skim through sleep that's snatched away as soon as it begins. Richard's moving, rolling me away. He gets up and crawls down the canes into the open.

"What're you doing?"

"Looking for your dress."

I brush the earth off me and go out after him. He's sweeping the ground with his hands, but every patch of shadow looks like something that's fallen.

"What if you don't find it?"

"I'll find it."

He scoops, pouncing. "Here it is."

There's enough light for us to see each other's pale nakedness. He lifts the dress and shakes it out. Then he crouches down with the dress between his hands.

"What are you doing? Richard, what're you doing with my dress?" I hear him strain and grunt, and the soft cotton rips.

"You've torn my dress."

He laughs, turns the dress round, rips it again.

"You bastard."

"You don't mind. You don't really mind."

"What did you do that for?"

He kicks the dress away, stands up. "So you can't go back in the house."

"I'll tear up your bloody jeans, then."

"You can't. They're too strong."

"You'll find out."

We grapple, swaying. Suddenly I slip my hands down and squeeze his balls, hard.

"Christ, Nina! That hurts."

"You don't mind," I say, "you like me hurting you."

"I like everything you do," he says.

"Isn't that nice."

"Wait a minute." He tenses, his body concentrating inward the way men do while they check if they're getting an erection or not.

"No, not now you've ripped up my dress."

"I'll get you another one."

"You won't. I buy my own clothes."

"I want you to be naked."

"It's dark. You can't see me."

"That doesn't matter."

*   *   *

I don't often get to the point where I forget who I am. Where I end, where the other person begins. You have to go on for a long time, and it's not a matter of emotions, it's a physical thing. I got there with Richard.

"We can't go inside like this," I say later. "We smell of fucking."

"You could put on my shirt."

"That'd be worse than nothing, wouldn't it. I know. Come on." I pull him with me toward Isabel's new apple trees. I feel the zinc bucket with my foot, see the faint shine of water.

"Stand still. Now, whatever I do, don't make a sound. Shut your eyes." I can't see if he shuts them or not. I bend, taking the weight of the heavy bucket with my thigh muscles. The water heaves up one side. "Bend down."

I stand very close to him, hoist up the bucket as high as I can, and tip it over us both, as slowly as I can, so that water runs in a cold, steady stream over thighs and shoulders and breasts.

"Wash me with it," I say, and keep on pouring while he lathers the water over me.

"Wait a minute. Open your legs."

"I've had enough, Richard."

"I'm only going to wash you." He scoops a handful of water, washes my vulva as gently and quickly as a nurse. "Now, you do me." I pass him the half-full bucket and then I wash his penis, his balls, the sweat and semen trapped in his hair.

"There, you're clean."

Richard dresses slowly, while I watch.

"Come on, put this round you. You'll get cold."

I put on his shirt and button it. It's long enough to cover my thighs, and if I meet anyone, why should they guess it doesn't belong to me?

"What time is it?"

"Eleven."

"Only eleven?"

"Yes. Nina . . ."

I can hear it in his voice, the talk that's got to come.

"I'm tired, Richard, I want to get to bed."

"I know. But there are things we've got to sort out. I'm away tomorrow."

"I told you I don't want to talk."

"Nina," he says, holding my wrists, "it's not going to work like that. Fucking in the garden and nothing in the house. You're kidding yourself. I know what your cervix feels like, for Christ's sake. I've watched you pissing. I'm fucked if we're not going to talk."

Cervix, I think briefly, impressed. As an index of intimacy, not many men would think of that. There was that TV program where blindfolded men had to pin the clitoris onto a drawing of a woman's fanny. Like pinning the tail on a donkey, only they weren't as accurate. One got it right, more or less right, and came out tapping the side of his nose. *Married man,* he said. I love things like that. Then I remember that of course Richard knows about cervices. There was Isabel's, opening up to give birth.

"Then I'm going back to London," I say.

He lets go of my wrists so abruptly my hands slap against my thighs, and walks away a few feet. I wait. At last he says in a dry, different voice, "You certainly are sisters, aren't you."

"What do you mean?"

"You give with one hand and you take back with the other."

I pull his shirt round me. "I'm going in."

"Go on, then."

Edward's waiting for me as I come through the kitchen door in the dark.

"I thought you'd come this way," he says. All my blood runs back to my heart, then shocks up to my skin. Edward turns on the light and the room leaps out at me, too bright, too shiny, every surface as inquisitive as Margery Wilkinson's eyes. I look down and see dark stains on the shirt I'm wearing, like blood. Raspberry juice. My legs are scratched too, and there's dirt on them.

"I knew already," says Edward. "I saw you this morning. Who do you think you are? You're not in the

chapter *sixteen*

THE LAMP IS ON and Isabel is standing by the baby's bed, sideways to me as I open the door. The drop bars are down. First I notice the big roses on her silk kimono, then her head, bent, her whole body leaning down over the child. Her hand is on him, pressing him. It seems as if all her weight is going down on him.

I open my dry mouth and my voice rasps in my throat. I see her, tall Isabel, her dark silky hair falling like bunches of grapes, her kimono brushing the floor. But I see another Isabel as well, half her height, in a cotton nightdress that comes down to her knees. This Isabel is braced, on tiptoe, leaning over the baby. Her hair is pushed back behind her ears, and I can see her thin, intent face. She is pressing down on the baby's back, pressing and pressing, pushing him into the mattress. I can see his weak purple legs thrashing, but there's no sound. His face is hidden in a muslin cloth. She hears me come in, she turns, she does not stop pushing the baby

Garden of fucking Eden, you know. I wish y
have seen yourself."

"Sex isn't meant to be pretty for onlooker
"You should know that. Or maybe you don't,
would've stayed more than an hour."

"I can't believe you're Isabel's sister."

"No, you're right. I'm not at all like Isabel. I'm
she's good, so bear it in mind." I tell myself i
touch me, none of this touches me. It's a gam
tennis. But my back's against the door and I'
breath.

"How can you do this to her?" he asks, and
there's no malice in it. He simply wants to kno
just had a baby. She's been terribly ill. You kn
vulnerable she is, or if you don't you should. D
ally not care about Isabel at all?"

"You don't have the right to ask me that."

And I know I've won. He looks away, flushir
his fine skin.

"There's something missing in you," he say
at him, but I can't make myself angry with hi
make myself feel any of the emotions he expects
wants. He does love Isabel.

"So what are you going to do?" I ask, and as l
he doesn't answer. I move toward the door. I c
Isabel now, asleep or not, before anyone else do
all, I'm her sister.

down. Her face is cold and hard, like a snake's face, but her voice is a soft whisper.

"He was crying. I'm getting him to sleep. Go back to our room."

And I go. I creep back on bare feet that are suddenly cold, across the linoleum to the big bed I share with Isabel. I climb in and wrap the sheets tightly round me, and I lie in the dark I've made, shivering until I fall asleep. When I wake up it's sunshine and morning and Isabel is on the floor, cross-legged, reading a book. She looks up and smiles at me.

The image switches off. Tall Isabel, my sister with her baby, stands by the cot patting her baby's back gently and rhythmically.

"He's got wind," she whispers. "He's had awful colic this evening."

"Isabel." I can't think of anything else to say.

"What's the matter?"

"Colin. What happened? What happened to Colin?"

But Isabel's golden face is smooth, glinting with peace. Cautiously, so as not to wake the baby, she stands back. I see Antony's perfect, sleeping face.

"What's wrong with you, Nina? You know he died of cot-death. I can't believe how you keep going on about it when I've just had Antony. I told Edward about it and he wanted to have a word with you, but I told him not to." She smiles. "Isn't it wonderful when they're asleep."

Waves of peaceful conspiracy wash over me, but this time I'm going to struggle. "Isabel, when I saw you there —" No, that isn't the way. "Isabel. The night Colin died. You must think back, it's important."

"I remember it," says Isabel. Her clear blue eyes look back at me, and there's a delicate frown cut into her forehead.

"Were you in his room? Before I woke up?"

"Was I in his room? What do you mean?"

"I mean, did you go into Colin's room? Did you stand by his cot, just like that, like you were standing by Antony's?"

"Why do you think that?" asks Isabel quickly.

"I saw it just now. You were standing there in your nightdress, the rosy nightdress. You remember, yours was pink and mine was blue. You turned round and spoke to me. You told me you were just getting the baby to sleep. 'Go back to our room,' that's what you said."

"What do you mean, you saw it?"

"I saw it. I remembered it. You know how I remember things in pictures."

She is silent, gazing back at me out of her untroubled face. But I know Isabel too well not to see the thoughts that race, flicker, dive, and surface again. She takes a step toward me, then another. Suddenly the rose silk of the kimono is round me, folding me in. Isabel is breathing hard, her breath working up into sobs. I pull away and see that there are tears on her face and more welling at the corners of her eyes.

"Oh Nina. Oh Neen," she stammers, her fine hands clasping mine. "I thought you'd really forgotten. I thought you wouldn't ever remember."

"But I do remember."

"Don't, Neen. Don't, don't. Don't remember. You were only four. It wasn't your fault. You didn't know what you were doing." Her big eyes swim at me, her face yearning with pity for me. I step back.

"What? What do you mean, Isabel? Of course it wasn't my fault. How could it have been my fault?"

"Do you remember everything?" she demands. She has the face of a compassionate judge.

"Of course I do." But uncertainty runs round me like ice, taking me into a new climate. Through the fog and cold I'm beginning to see the bulk of Isabel's truth, advancing like an iceberg to blot out my world.

"You were only four," she explains. "You were jealous, of course you were. It was natural. That's why I never made a fuss of Colin, or held him — you must remember that, Neen. Everyone thought it was strange, because I'd loved holding you when you were a baby. But I knew you hated it when I touched him. That's why Mum didn't go on breast-feeding him, because you were so jealous. She thought it'd make you feel better if he had bottles."

"You didn't want to hold him," I say.

"Of course I did. I always loved babies. Then that night — do you remember? — you got into trouble because you were jumping on the bed and making a noise and you woke him up. Mum was furious. I tried to make you feel better, but I didn't realize how upset you were really. Then we must have fallen asleep."

"But you were in the bedroom," I say. "You were leaning over his cot."

"Of course I was, but that was afterward."

"After what?"

"After I came in and found Colin. I'd heard you come back in the room, and I thought you'd been to the toilet. But then I woke up properly, and I knew you couldn't have, because you were frightened of the cistern, so you always woke me up to take you. So I thought something must be wrong. You were very cold, so I wrapped you up in bed again. But you'd left the door open. I went to shut it and I saw Colin's door was open as well. I went in and I found what you'd done. The pillow was still over his head."

I stare at Isabel, unable to speak.

"I knew they'd know it was you. Everyone had said how jealous you were. I took off the pillow and turned him over, and I knew he was dead because of the color he'd gone. I arranged all the blankets again and put him so he looked as if he was asleep, facing the door. But when I turned round, you were there. You hadn't gone back to sleep. I didn't want to frighten you, so I told you Colin had woken up and I was settling him. I didn't want you to know what you'd done. I thought you'd never know. You might have forgotten it all in the morning."

I lick my lips. "I didn't remember," I say in a crack of a voice.

"I knew you didn't. I could tell that in the morning. So after we'd played I pretended to go and see how Colin was. I wanted you not to think it had anything to do with you."

"Isabel." Fear, horror, admiration, disbelief, fight in me. The iceberg slices the side of my ship, and I go down. But though I'm finished, Isabel doesn't seem to know it, and her voice patters on.

"That's why I was ill. I had to keep it all in and not tell anyone. I couldn't go to the funeral."

"You've never, then . . . you've never . . . told anyone?"

"No," she says, holding my eyes, "of course not. I've never blamed you, Neen. I'll never blame you for anything. I love you."

chapter seventeen

NOBODY KNOWS. Not Richard, not Edward. She hasn't told anyone because it was too dangerous. I was her Neen, her baby. She thought they'd take me away if they knew.

She loved me so much, I always knew that. I always knew that Isabel loved me even more than my mother did, because she told me so. Often she walked me right to the end of Smeaton's pier, when the tide was high and the fishing boats were coming into harbor. We could look down through twenty feet of water that was as clear as jelly. If we fell we'd hang there like fruit in jelly. The wind blew, our hair flapped, and she held my hand tight. The fall we might have fallen made my knees ache, but I was safe with Isabel. My mother would let her take me anywhere.

"I've had to hide it all for so long. I'm sorry, Neen. I'm so, so sorry. If you hadn't said anything, I'd never have told you. But I swear I'll never tell anyone else."

"Not even Richard?"

"No."

And the evidence. She didn't need to tell me what would have happened to the evidence. All dissolved now, vanished underground. Colin's been buried so long. No one found any evidence then, and they never would now.

"Did the police come?" I ask. Isabel shakes her head so her hair gleams and ripples in the lamplight. Why am I thinking of how beautiful she is, now, when it's the last thing that counts?

"The doctor came."

"Did he ask us what happened?"

"Of course not. We weren't the ones who'd found Colin. We'd been asleep all night, just like we usually were."

"And you didn't — you never said anything to them?"

A tiny, sideways movement of Isabel's head. She watches me intently. "Are you all right, Neen? You look awful."

"I'm — I don't know. I don't feel like me anymore."

"It's because it was a shock. You didn't realize before. You never knew anything. I always knew you didn't." She smiles fluently at me, offering me back my innocence. "You could never have pretended so well. You know how they say children bury memories deep down, if something terrible happens."

"I must have known. You can't do something like that and not know it." I circle round the words that I can't bring myself to say. A four-year-old girl, me, put a pillow over the head of a baby and pressed down until he was dead, then she went back into her room and slept until morning. And never said anything about it, or did anything, or remembered anything. Why don't my hands remember? Why don't my fingers ache? He must have struggled.

"You remember the games we used to play with our dolls?" says Isabel. "They were always being ill and dying and having funerals then coming back to life. You must have thought that would happen to Colin. You only did to him what you'd done to your doll lots of times. You didn't really know what death was."

But I did. I went to the funeral and saw him come out in that little white box in our father's arms. The lid was down, fastened down, and it would never be taken off. I understood that, and I was afraid when I looked at my mother's terrible face. I knew something about death.

"Isabel." My voice scrapes. "Thank you." Isabel's eyes widen.

"Thank you? What for?"

"Not saying anything."

"I'll never say anything. You can trust me, Neen."

150

I stare at her. The thought ripples in me that even if she did say something now, no one would believe her. There is no evidence, so it's Isabel's word against mine. Even my mother is firmly dead, and I think that only she could ever dare to put together the threads of such a story.

"Go to bed," says Isabel. "Go to sleep, Neen. You look worn out."

My sister stares deep into my eyes. Her body is a column of calm, and there is still a tiny half smile on her face. All I've been thinking about since I got here is her weakness, her fragility, but now that is stripped away and it's easy to see how strong she really is. She's said nothing for twenty-five years. And not only that, she's never changed toward me. I try to think what it must be like to take the hand of a four-year-old who's killed her baby brother and lead her back to bed. Without frightening me. And then taking away the pillow, and rearranging Colin to lie "as if he was asleep."

I wonder what would have happened if Isabel hadn't thought so quickly? I would have had a different life, not my own life. What life I possess, I possess because Isabel's given it to me. Isabel is my mother.

"I'll see you in the morning," says Isabel. "Go to sleep. We won't ever talk about it again. It'll be the same as it's always been."

There's a tiny sigh, a huff of breath from Antony's bed.

*   *   *

I sleep. I am by the sea, the wind blowing, the rage of gulls in my ears. We're climbing cliffs, too high. The noise of the gulls changes into angry voices above my head. I am small and half-hidden in my mother's skirt, standing in the cold, blowing street while the adults talk over me.

"I've said to myself many a time seeing your girl pass, she's too young to be let out with that pram. If Jos Quick hadn't made a grab for it, your littl'un ud have been a goner."

My mother, cold, clipped: "It was an accident. She's very sorry."

"I daresay. She was poking about there in the floats and nets, did you know that? Had her back to the pram, though she'd gone and left it right on the edge of the pier with the brake off. Did she tell you that?"

"Of course she did."

"She wants her backside tanned, if you ask me. How old is she? Seven? Old enough to know better."

"It won't happen again."

The voices change. They are gulls now, not women. One of them hurtles down the air toward me, braking just above my head. I feel its claws in my hair, tangling, dragging, lifting, to carry me away with it to its carrion nest on the cliffs. I wake with an icy jolt to my watch showing 4:17. The dream is so clear that I put my hand to my hair. But the voices are fading already, becoming noise, not words. A few seconds after I come out of the dream it has dissolved.

But I'm not out of sleep yet. The dream has given way to another dream. My mother stays. She isn't angry anymore, but I can see her sitting on my bed, crossing her legs with a faint rasp of nylon. She must be going out somewhere, because for work she wears trousers and a smock and she smells of clay dust, not gardenia. It's evening and I'm ready for bed, but Isabel hasn't come upstairs yet. My legs are long now, and my feet make a bump well down the bedclothes. I'm seven or eight. My mother looks at me and says, "I've always known I can leave my purse anywhere in the house and you and Isabel won't touch it." And I nod, proud, enthralled with the idea of my own honesty. "Never mind, Nina," she says.

"Never mind what?"

"It was just —" she looks carefully away, "just I thought I had more money than I found I had, when I came to pay the milkman."

"You must have spent it already."

"Yes, I must." She reaches over to the funny lock of hair that always flops over my face unless I stab it firmly with a hairpin. She strokes the hair back.

"Is my hair nearly as long as Isabel's?" I ask.

"Not quite." My mother is always truthful. Sometimes I think less truth would make our life more comfortable.

"Is anything worrying you, Nina?" asks my mother, suddenly, surprising me. This is not her sort of question.

"No. Of course not." I make my eyes as honest as I can in the semidark.

"I just thought that sometimes . . . it might be difficult for you, having Isabel . . . having an elder sister ahead of you all the time."

"You mean, because Isabel's so good at everything."

"Not only that."

I try to think what my mother can possibly mean. Of course Isabel is better than me at school, but I'm used to that. Teachers remember Isabel all the way up the school, and when I arrive in the class they're ready for me. I'm haunted by the ghost of her perfect copying, and by the neat way her socks stay up. I have been shown pages of Isabel's exercise books with her sums done so beautifully that the teacher has given her not only ten red stars but a silver rabbit to stick onto the book.

"Because she's got longer hair and everything?"

"Mm. No. I just wondered if you wanted to do more things on your own. Without Isabel."

"I like being with Isabel."

"I know you do. But you like drawing and Isabel doesn't."

"I always do drawing while Isabel's busy."

"Yes. But you're quite good at drawing. It won't develop unless you work on it."

My mother sounds as if she's talking to a grown-up, not me. I wriggle round in the bed. "You could give us lessons," I suggest. I know that my mother doesn't mean Isabel and me, she means just me, but perversely I don't want to acknowledge that. Isabel can draw a vase of daisies and a cat watching a goldfish. And that's that. People at school hang over her desk when she does them.

"Isabel's going to tea with Katie Trevose tomorrow. Why don't you come then?" She shifts her weight. I know she'll only ask me once, because that's how my mother is. She never tries to persuade us.

"All right."

"Good." She pats my legs. I slide down in the bed, silent. Isabel will be coming to bed in a minute. Will she be able to smell my treachery in the air?

I am awake now. Really awake. I have got to think what to do. It's later than I thought; I must have fallen asleep again. It's ten to six and the room is light. I'm hungry.

No one else is up yet, not even the baby. There's

155

nothing in the cupboards. Instant coffee, two packets of Weetabix, cheap jelly marmalade. Isabel grows her own vegetables, but she also has a freezer full of white sliced bread and beef sausages. I reach into the hollow china duck where keys are kept. Yes, Richard's left his car keys.

It's nice to be back in a car, in its city smell of used-up air. I click on the radio, turn on the ignition and reverse carefully round the pond. As I come out onto the track I have the feeling I'm being watched. I keep on, driving faster than I should on the rough surface, not looking back.

Town's empty too. I park the car and walk down Wash Street toward the corner where I remember a bakery. I can smell it already, the warmth of new bread curling out into the gray streets. The gray is thinning to blue, and it'll be hot again, of course. It takes so little time to get used to a climate where the sun always shines.

It's a good bakery. I buy cheese bread and a wheel of fresh pizza in a white cardboard box, two French sticks and a sticky dark loaf with sunflower seeds in it. I buy a box of homemade shortbread, and five cream-filled doughnuts. Susan, Richard, Edward, Nina. And Isabel. The assistant finds bags and packs the stuff in. I add a pot of ginger chutney, and just then the first batch of croissants comes in on a stained metal tray and I buy twelve. I walk out, my arms, full, peering over bags and boxes. A man walking his dog smiles at me. "You've a family to feed, all right," he says, and I nod and smile and imagine the person who might go home to the scrubbed wooden table and the Aga and the scrubbed blond children and dump the parcels on the table saying breathlessly, "Now darlings, don't all grab at once. . . ."

I stow the bags and get into the car. The streets are clean and empty, and I drive on a rush of exhilaration, out of the town, accelerating onto the wide white road that curves past the bottom of the Downs. The sun is up and there are fresh blue shadows at the side of the road. Over the Downs the sky is shining, and the car smells of bread and pizza. The radio's playing *Turn your back on me* . . . and then a truck grows huge in the mirror, all metal teeth so close up I think it's going to hit, until at the last moment it swings out. Its wheels thud the road alongside me, jouncing the car, taking up the whole road as a blind corner comes up fast. Its brakes hiss enormously but it keeps going, trundling beside me in a blind thunder of weight and speed. The moment stretches, the huge wheels churn in the window-space beside me, so close I could put out my hand. But nothing happens. No car coming the other way, no moment where being alive explodes into . . . what? Nothing happens. I hold the wheel tight. The windows are wide open and I hear a bird sing in the hedge on my left. Then the truck rocks in ahead of me, straightens, drives on. I am less than half a mile from the turnoff to the track.

I turn off, and stop the car. The birds sing louder. I feel no different this morning from any other morning. It hasn't sunk in, I tell myself. I am still living as if I don't know the truth of what I am. The morning world is as new and shiny as it's ever been. The track ahead of me bulges with cows' backsides as they walk slowly, willingly, and I put the car into gear and drive behind, at their pace.

Richard's in the kitchen, giving the baby his bottle. I carry in all my bags and boxes, and kick the door shut. He looks at me but says nothing. The baby is crumpled and tiny against his blue shirt. Richard looks up at me, but his face is hard to read.

"Breakfast," I say, dumping everything on the table.

"Smells good."

"It'll be good. The only thing I couldn't get was coffee."

"There's a jar in the cupboard."

"I'm sure there is. I'm talking about coffee."

"You're a snob, did you know that? A food snob."

Our conversation is as tinny as an advert. I go over and stand close to him, and the baby looks up, but not at us. It occurs to me suddenly that you could do anything you liked in front of a baby. It frightens me to think of the power that comes with the birth of a child.

"He's drinking it."

"Of course he is," says Richard. "He's already had two bottles in the night. I'm sorry to say it, but Susan's mother was right. He was hungry."

"She's a bitch."

"But sexy, don't you think? Unlike Susan."

"Susan's sexy."

"Not as sexy as you."

"Jesus, Richard, why are we having such a crap conversation at this time of the morning?"

"I don't know. I find it hard to know what to say to you."

I put croissants onto plates, find some raspberry jam in the cupboard, cut bread, and get a clean, pale slab of butter out of the fridge.

"It's nice watching you," says Richard. "You ran off last night."

"You were pushing me."

I watch his hand holding the bottle, his broad thumb under the nipple. I love how experienced he looks.

"Were you watching me from the window this morning, when I drove off?"

"No."

"I thought someone was."

"Might have been Isabel. She didn't sleep, that's why I'm giving Ant here his bottles."

Ant. He says it with casual affection, as if for the first time the baby's a real person to him. And then he smiles down at the baby and says, "You're doing all right on this stuff, aren't you?"

"I'll take him," I say, and hold out my arms. "You can make the coffee."

Richard lifts the drowsy, wobbling baby. I take him, putting two fingers to support his neck. A burp of milk runs out of his mouth and he sneezes, then falls asleep, hanging from my hands like a kitten. I ease him into the crook of my arm and stare down at him as Richard moves around the kitchen, taking mugs off hooks and filling the kettle. How light he is. How easy it would be to hurt him. But is being afraid of how easy it would be the same thing as wanting to do it? Layers of wanting and not wanting look into themselves like mirrors. I don't want to hurt him, but I'm afraid of wanting to hurt him. Just one finger over his nostrils would do it. And there's his pulse, bumping away in the tender center of his head. It makes me dizzy to think how easy it would be to hurt him. He is curled in on himself, trusting the world to hold him because he has no other choice. I think of the children in the orphanage in Romania, reaching out for their drums and tambourines. They have no choice either. If any light shines, they have to turn toward it. But there's an instinct, surely there's an instinct that keeps us from doing a baby harm? Children burn with jealousy but they don't do anything. Even a jealous, raging four-year-old can tell the difference between her brother and a doll. I was a child and innocent. I never cut worms in half, or stamped on flies.

But my dolls were always alive to me. They had moods and dreams. They could be hurt and then comforted. That was the magic power we had, me and Isabel. We were their parents and we were omnipotent. I've put out of my mind some of those games we played.

"Richard."

"What?"

"Do you ever feel frightened — you know, when you're holding him — in case you drop him?"

"All the time. I'm glad to hear women do as well."

"But you get used to it."

"It doesn't take long, does it? Look at you."

I look at myself. A young woman in her sister's kitchen, holding her baby nephew while her brother-in-law makes coffee. The baby sleeps peacefully, and the young woman's fingers curl protectively around his head.

"They're tougher than you think, anyway," says Richard. "Isabel dropped him once and it didn't seem to do much harm."

"God, did she really? When was that?" I feel curiously relieved. If even Isabel —

"Just after she got back from hospital. She was very shaky. I came in and there he was on the floor with poor Isabel on her knees trying to pick him up. She was in a terrible state."

He planks a mug of coffee down in front of me.

"Don't put it there, Richard."

"It's okay. He can't grab stuff yet."

"I just keep thinking of things like the coffee spilling on his head."

"It won't." But he moves the mug. "What you're afraid of never happens," he says. "It's the things you don't think of that happen." Then he comes round behind me, pulls my head back, lets his fingers slide round my cheek, my jaw, my throat. He finds textures in me that were never there before.

"Are you going out later?"

"Yes."

"Where?"

"The river."

"I'll get you a croissant. Stay there."

I eat it with my eyes shut: the jam, the cold, salty butter, the warm, dissolving layers of pastry. He feeds it into my mouth inch by inch, and I eat it down to the crisp, burnt point.

"I'll come," he says. "What time?"

"About three."

"You'll be there."

"Of course I will."

You don't know who you're talking to, I think.

chapter *eighteen*

THERE IS A WAY out to the water meadows through
the garden. It's a little door cut into the side wall, covered with creepers. Hard to see if you're not looking. It
isn't locked, and outside there are planks laid over what
would be boggy ground any summer but this. No water
now, only pale, dry grass. I shut the door behind me, the
door Isabel didn't find the first time she came to her garden. Edward's gone to London for the day. I should be
there too, but I'm not going. I had two calls this morning about the Romanian job, one to fix dates, the other
to sort out a meeting as soon as possible. I wanted to go.
While I was talking into the phone I felt like a different
person, quick and definite, someone who knew how to
think her way around a project as well as how to take
the pictures and do the drawings. They need to meet me
soon. I have to plan how I'll respond to what's going on
before it's all happening in front of me in a foreign language.

I've put them off, even though I could hear seeds of

doubt about me lodge as I talked. Maybe they hadn't made such a good choice after all. I told them how ill my sister is, how young the baby is, and that a nanny's coming in starting next week. Even while I was lying, it was still nice to hear voices from that other world, with other phones ringing in the background and the tap of our conversation being noted into a word processor while it was going on. I heard the impatience of people who aren't much interested in personal things. I didn't like it, but I knew it, I felt at home with it. That's what I'll go back to when this is over.

Isabel is the same to me as ever today, as she said she would be. She's said nothing. I made a green salad with the pizza for lunch, and put the cream doughnuts in the fridge for later. Isabel smoked cigarette after cigarette all morning, wandering around the house with a mug of coffee in her other hand. She didn't seem to know what to do without Edward.

"You shouldn't drink so much of that stuff," I said. She buys cheap powdered coffee from the village shop, in white tins without a name on them.

"It's okay. I've stopped feeding the baby," she said, as if the only thing that mattered was what went into the baby's milk. It's a sharp, sudden change. Isabel's cast him off. She doesn't want to give him his bottle, and Susan's spent most of the morning feeding him, burping him, feeding him again. The new milk hurts his stom-

ach. He cries and belches, then cries while yellow
streams of sick flow down his babygrows. The air is full
of tobacco smoke and screaming. Richard watched Isabel as she tapped out her ash, frowning, listened for the
baby, walked on. Her breasts are big and full and hurting. She kept saying she wanted the doctor to give her
something to stop the milk. Richard's face was so heavy
with trouble that I wanted to shout at him, "For God's
sake, don't let her see you looking like that."

It's good to shut the door on it and be out. The meadows are cracked with drought, and there are bald
patches where the cattle have trampled away the grass.
There are hundreds of tiny pale blue butterflies, more
than there've ever been, Susan says, a plague of butterflies. They don't fly, they vibrate in the heat. It's hotter
now than it was at noon. You can't imagine anything else
but this, day after day, going on and on without cloud
or breeze. The heat builds its own silence. It cuts us off
as surely as a flood. Walking through the field I feel like
a dot in so much summer. The trees look as if they've
been suspended, let down through the air on invisible
strings. Crickets chirr as I walk down the field, so
fiercely that it becomes another landscape, not England.
The fields are white and cracked, the sky a sharp, de-
manding blue. From here you can't see the river, but
when I've crossed two more fields I'll be there. Which
way will Richard come? He can't cross the fields, be-

cause anyone could see him from the house. They can see me now, if they want to. Isabel can, or Susan. I've bought a larger sketchbook, and it's wedged under my arm where anyone can see it. A big, portable excuse for everything. They can see me now. Nina, full of pizza, plodding over the water meadows. It takes her forever. My back braces itself, and a trickle of sweat gathers between my shoulders and runs slowly down. The cattle are bunched up by the hedge, in what shade there is.

I reach the water. It's not what I wanted. It isn't cool, or brown, or alive with fish and shadows. It is a strange porcelain green with a thick current down the middle, and a few clumps of willow and alder gripping tight to its banks. There is hardly any shade here either. Heat bounces off the water into my eyes. The towpath is narrow, and because the river is slightly above the level of the meadows, there is an uneasy feeling that everything has got into the wrong place. I stand and watch the water bulging round the reeds on its way downstream. It hasn't got far to go now, only five miles to the sea. It's packed with chemicals, effluent, the runoff from miles of farmland. The quality of the water is better than it was, Richard says, but no one paddles or swims here now. No one comes here much. What is there but a high, exposed path along the snakes of the river. It bends like a river in a child's storybook, not a real river. I can't see the bottom. I remember Richard saying once, "It's deep.

Be careful, those banks are chalk and they crumble. The current's stronger than it looks." I stare into the water. I would not want to choke in that soup of chemicals. The water doesn't smell, exactly, but it gives off a strange, metallic tang. I look up and down the banks, but for miles there's nowhere hidden, nowhere we can tuck ourselves away out of sight and fuck ourselves insensible.

I sit down carefully, folding my legs under me. I watch a twig sail down the current, surprisingly fast. I open my sketchbook and take out my pencil, though there's nothing here I want to draw. Except perhaps those willow roots, the hunch and clench of them, like hands digging into soil. I move a little, turn the book round, squeeze my eyes to filter out glare.

I draw for a long time. In the middle of the drawing I realize without needing to think about it that I've stopped expecting Richard to come. Good. I'm fighting the temptation to make these roots more than roots, to turn them into the hands they aren't. Roots work differently. I rip off a sheet of spoiled paper, and I'm about to crumple it into a ball and shove it in my pocket when I have a better idea. I smooth out the paper and fold it. One fold, a turn, another fold. A triangle. A cocked hat. A little boat.

I daren't go down the white, crumbling bank. I throw the boat out. Too heavy to flutter, it turns in the air, then amazingly it rights itself, falls on the water, and begins to sail. A current whips it from underneath, and it spins, then straightens, and sails on fast down the center of the river. I watch it until it disappears round the next bend, out of sight before it can become water-logged and sink.

I'm still staring after it when there's a huge distur-bance behind me. I think of great sheets of paper being ripped in the sky. I turn. Something big and baggy-winged stretches itself up from the river behind the next clump of willows. It hauls itself up into the air, hardly gaining any height. Like a dream of flying when you will yourself over hedges, it goes over me low, so low I duck, and find myself on hands and knees on the path. And then it picks up speed with great flaps of its wings. Slowly, more slowly than I'd ever thought a bird could rise, it climbs the sky. It shows with its broad, ragged wings what hard work flying is. All this time I'm holding my breath because it nearly doesn't work.

"A heron! Did you see it?" shouts Richard from across the meadow. He's coming straight down, the way I came, so anyone can see him coming. He strides up, wiping sweat from his face. "Did you see that! There must be fish in the river after all."

"I can't believe that," I say, looking into its poison-ous green depths.

"Jesus, it's hot." He looks around, as I've done, regis-ters the lack of shade and shelter, as I've done. The walk's been too much for him. I see suddenly and coolly how much the weight and age he carries slow him down. He sits heavily beside me, and though I want to go on drawing I put down my pencil. It is much too hot for me to want to touch him. I think he must feel the same.

"Sometimes I think this place is the arse end of nowhere," says Richard.

"I know what you mean."

"But Isabel loves it."

We stare out past the polluted water to the baking meadows opposite.

"This is hell," says Richard. "Let's walk. It can't be worse than sitting here."

We walk one behind the other to the bend in the river. Ahead of us are more bends, winding away to the sea between flat meadows. On the far right there's a concrete building that looks like an electricity substation. In the distance the Downs bake, almost hidden by heat haze.

"Do you want to walk on?"

"Not really."

He laughs. "This is awful, isn't it? What are we doing here?"

"I was drawing."

"But it's better than being in the house," says Richard. I look at him. This sounds like the most intimate thing he's ever said to me.

"How are things back there?"

"Isabel's missing Edward."

"He's only been gone four hours."

"I know. But she needs someone to talk to. She isn't feeling too good at the moment."

We let pass, silently, the fact that she talks to neither of us.

"And Susan's fucked off to help her mother with this Young Farmers do."

"What?"

"I said Susan's gone over to the farm. Why, what's the matter?"

"You mean now? She's there now? She's not with Isabel?" I've swung round to face Richard. My hands are on his elbows, gripping them. "You mean Isabel's on her own?"

"Susan's only over at the farm. She'll be back by five. And Isabel's got the baby, so she's not really on her own."

"The baby's with Isabel?"

"Nina, for God's sake, of course the baby's with Isabel. *What's the matter with you?*"

The heat pours on my head.

"When did Susan go?"

"I don't know, the same time as me. Yes, I saw her leave. Nina, what is all this? Isabel's fine. I wouldn't have left her if she wasn't. Nina! Where're you going?"

I scramble down the bank and into the meadow.

"Nina!"

"She shouldn't be left on her own! It's too soon!" I shout back. There are three fields and the garden between me and Isabel. I begin to run.

I am faster than Richard. I glance back and see him coming after me, thumping the dry ground, but I run faster. I've got to get there first, before anyone else sees. My feet slide on their own sweat inside my sandals. I am gasping, but I know I can run much farther than this. I climb the first stile, and drop back onto the path. The quickest way is straight across the fields. If she looks through the window, if she sees me coming, running over the fields like this, then she'll wait. She'll stand there watching, distracted, wondering what's going on. I shoot up one arm and wave madly to an invisible Isabel. *I'm coming! Stay there, don't move. Don't do anything.*

I bang the little door open. The garden's silent, stewing in heat and scent. Up the paths, hedges whipping my legs, and round the side and into the stale, dark kitchen. No one there. The back door open, the clock ticking. Down the passage, across the hall, up the stairs in silent, hungry bounds. She's there. She must be. I stand and listen, but I can't hear anything. The house is as quiet as if everyone's stopped breathing. Then I hear her singing. Her nice voice, thin but sweet:

My daddy was a preacher,
My daddy was a thief.
Eevy ivy overhead,
How many hours does the baby sleep?
Eevy ivy overhead . . .

I know it well. That song's lodged in my bones, like all the songs Isabel once sang me. She begins again, *My daddy was a preacher . . . ,* and all those summer evenings of Isabel's singing tumble back over me. I take in a breath. I am hot, shivering with heat. I hear Isabel stir inside the room, the chair creak, her footsteps light on the bare boards —

I open the door. Antony's bed is empty.

"Where's the baby?"

"The baby?" Isabel opens her eyes wide. I see the fringe of her lashes spray wide. Her eyes are clear as storybook rivers. "He's in Susan's room, of course. Fast asleep. For heaven's sake don't go in and wake him up. It took me forever to get him off."

"Oh. I thought you were singing to him."

"I wasn't singing."

"You were. I heard you."

"What, then? What was I singing?"

I purse my lips. I hate singing, even when I'm alone. Isabel could sing, I couldn't. "You were singing *How many hours does the baby sleep?*"

Isabel laughs. "I haven't thought of that for years, Neen." Her tense face is relaxing, slowly. "But where've you been?"

"Down by the river," I say quickly. "I was drawing."

"I know. I saw you go."

"Did you see Richard too? He came down, thinking it would be cooler, but it was even hotter by the river."

"Yes, I saw him." She turns aside, pulling at her dress. "Christ, look at this. I'm soaked in milk again."

"It'll stop soon, won't it?"

"Susan says so. She'd know, of course."

"Of course." Our eyes meet in shared amusement.

"Why doesn't she have one?" demands Isabel. "Why doesn't she just bloody well have one?"

"The same reason I don't," I say. "She doesn't want one."

"You do, Neen, of course you do," croons Isabel, dabbing milk off herself.

"I'm going to make some tea. There are those cream doughnuts in the fridge. Do you want any?"

Isabel glances up, her eyes sliding past mine. "Look in on the baby for me, Neen, on your way down. Just to check he's all right."

The sweat from my run chills all over me. I'm tangled

up as I was in her singing, tangled up in words I've heard before, in things that have happened once and should never happen again. Surely she knows what she's saying. Careless and intimate, that's how we look. Two sisters in a bedroom.

On your way down . . . just to check he's all right . . . go and look at the baby, Neen. Go and look at the baby.

chapter nineteen

SLOWLY, SLOWLY, I push open the door of Susan's room. I make no sound. The pale curtains are drawn, and the room smells of the new pine furniture, and baby sleep. He is rosy with the heat, his hair damp, his fist up to his face. He is sleeping on his side, and Isabel has put a rolled-up towel beside him so he can't turn onto his face. I creep right up to the cot. His weight dents the mattress. He looks more solid than I've ever seen him. Already he's changing, filling out, and that fist by his face looks strangely mature. He is sleeping peacefully in the thick yellow light that filters through Susan's curtains. All my fears sink down. He's well, perfectly well. I've been imagining things.

Richard is at the bottom of the stairs, looking up. "What was all that about? I couldn't keep up with you."

But he hasn't tried. He must have been waiting down there for a while, because he's not out of breath anymore. I wonder why he didn't come up after me. Perhaps he didn't want to break in on me and Isabel, but I doubt it. "She's a lot tougher than you think, you know," he says.

"I got worried about her being alone in the house. It was stupid." I stand on the bottom stair, and our eyes are almost on a level.

"You think of her more than she thinks of you," says Richard.

"I don't know how you can think that."

"Because I see things from the outside."

"You're wrong. Isabel's always been . . ." But it's hard to find words for what Isabel's always been.

"I think you need to get away from Isabel." He's entirely serious.

"How can you say that? She's my sister, she's always looked after me."

"Has she?"

"Richard, how can you talk like this about Isabel? You're married to her. She's my sister."

"It's got nothing to do with how I feel about Isabel. I know her very, very well. I know her much better than you do. I don't think you two do each other any good. Isabel knows what she wants, Nina."

"And I don't?"

"No. You don't let yourself. You're in a dream half the time."

It's the economist talking, the fulfillment man. The lens is on me and it's going to come zooming in. I start to gabble out a diversion. "I'm going to make some tea to take up to Isabel. The baby's asleep, so she's going to rest till he wakes up."

In the kitchen I make myself quick and busy, filling a tray with milk and mugs and plates. I take three doughnuts out of the fridge.

"Do you want one?"

"Why are you giving that to Isabel? She won't want it."

I lay Isabel's doughnut on a plate on the tray. It is puffy and light, covered with white and brown scribbles of icing.

"I'll eat it," says Richard, stretching out his hand.

"I bought enough for one each. That one in the bag's yours."

"But you know she doesn't —"

"She might."

The kettle boils, and I pour water into the pot. Richard puts his hand on the back of my knee. "Shit, Richard, this is boiling water."

"I know. But you've got steady hands. I've watched you." He slides his hand up, over my thigh, inside the cuff of my shorts.

I put down the kettle with my steady hands, but I don't turn. "I'll come down," I say. "I won't be long. I'll just take this up to Isabel."

"She doesn't sleep with me anymore, you know," says Richard.

"Of course she does. She got pregnant with Antony."

"That didn't take long. She'd got it worked out so it only took one go."

"You don't need to tell me any of that. I don't care."

"Because it's separate? That's the way you see it?"

"I don't see it any way."

"No, you don't, do you? We don't have to think, and we don't have to talk. Everything goes on in the dark. Well, that may be fine for you, but it isn't for me."

"Take your hand away if you don't like it."

His hand tightens on my thigh. "I'd love you to stand there naked, cooking," he says.

"With maybe a little apron?"

"I'm not that perverse."

"What would I cook?"

"I don't know. Anything. You'd be there chopping and stirring. Tasting things. You always taste when you cook, don't you?"

"I can't cook any other way."

"You'd have a wooden spoon in your mouth."

"And you'd watch."

"Oh no, I'd do more than that."

"Food's important. You don't want to go mixing it up with other things."

"You would, though, wouldn't you. You would, wouldn't you?"

Isabel's tray is cheap and buckled. The teapot slips, but I balance it and push her door open with my knee.

"Oh Neen, tea, lovely. Let me shove all this stuff off the table." She's been writing another letter. I pull up the other chair, and sit down opposite her.

"You don't still take sugar in tea, do you, Neen? It's bad for your skin."

"I need it after all that running."

"I saw you. What on earth was the matter? You tearing up the field and Richard chasing you. It looked as if he'd been trying it on down by the river." She laughs.

"You know, Isabel, how you said we weren't going to talk about last night — about what we talked about last night?"

"We're not," she answers quickly. "I said I wouldn't talk about it again, and I won't." This time it sounds like a declaration, not a reassurance.

"I want to. I've been thinking about it all night." I lean forward and begin to divide the two doughnuts into quarters with a sharp knife. I cut them very carefully so that the dough isn't squashed down on the cream. Isabel feels on her table for the cigarette pack, taps one out without looking, and lights it. I know how

Isabel smokes when there's food around, so that the cigarette makes a barrier between her and the plate. She can't put food in her mouth if there's a cigarette in it. I pour tea for us both.

"Why do you want to?" says Isabel.

"I went in to look at Ant just now. He was asleep. He looked so —"

"Peaceful."

"No. That's not the right word. I don't know how to describe it. He looked *there*. Solid. A hundred percent alive. And I thought, Colin must have looked like that. He's been dead such a long time I've been thinking of him as if he was never really alive. But he was. He was solid too."

Isabel draws sharply on her cigarette. "So?"

"And when I started to think about it, I couldn't believe that even when I was only four years old, I wouldn't have felt the difference. Between what you can do to a doll and what you can do to a baby."

"But Colin died." I watch the tidemark of milk on her dress, moving with her quick breath.

"Yes. But maybe it wasn't that way."

"I saw it. I know it was. I was seven, remember."

"It could have been an accident."

A breath goes out of Isabel, and her shoulders sink. She looks down, at the end of her cigarette, then up. "I suppose . . . I suppose it could have been." She frowns, thinking back. There's a little more color in her face now.

"I would have remembered killing him," I say. The words erupt in the room like vomit, and Isabel flinches.

"Don't say that."

"But that's what it means, doesn't it, if it wasn't an accident? It means I killed him. What else could have happened?"

"That's why you ran back," says Isabel. "You thought, if it could happen to Colin for no reason, then it could happen to Antony. Isn't that what it was? You were frightened. You were out of breath when you came in."

I look at her. Again Isabel's taken what's happened and made it a different truth that I can't argue with. "Yes, I suppose it was."

"But I'm sure I saw what I saw," Isabel goes on, frowning more deeply.

"It's not just what you see, though, is it? It's what you make of what you see. You have to interpret things."

And then it comes to me. I don't just see it, I see and I know. Colin's legs were moving. Bare, purple, weak legs beating up and down on the mattress as Isabel bent over the cot. *I saw that*. Could I have made it up? Made myself see movement where there was only stillness? Could I have been so terrified of what I'd done that I not only hid it from myself forever, but made up another scene, one where Isabel stood over the baby and the baby was alive, half-hidden by her body, struggling? Have I made those pictures in my mind, frame by frame? Isabel stood by the cot while I watched from the door. And she leaned down, pressed down.

I could have invented it all. I might be capable of that. How am I going to find out what I'm capable of? I stare at my golden sister.

"Don't worry, Neen. Everything's all right." Isabel looks at me as if we've said all we need to say. I feel trapped, overwhelmed. I know nothing, and I can't trust my own memory. Isabel is so sure.

"We've never been all that happy, you know," she says.

"What?"

"Me and Richard. It's been difficult for a long time."

I wrench my mind round to this. "You and Richard?"

She nods, and I believe her. The mystery of Isabel and Richard used to be one of my touchstones. That was the way you could be, if you found the right person. I thought they possessed a happiness they hid to keep it safe from outsiders. They were the adults, the ones who knew how life worked.

"No, it was never much good." She stares straight at me, shrugging off everything. "And now I can't bear it. I can't have him near me." She stubs out her cigarette. "Are those doughnuts nice, Neen?"

"They're fantastic. Really light, not greasy at all."

183

Isabel hesitates. I feel her wanting, but I don't know what she wants. Was there a time once, before she'd coached herself out of hunger, that we could stand in front of the baker's shop together and point at cream slices and Eccles cakes and eclairs? Was there a time when we'd both watch jealously as the tinned pineapple was divided, piece by piece, until our bowls were exactly equal?

"Go on," I say. "You know you're hungry." Isabel stretches out her long, delicate hand. She picks up a quarter of iced doughnut, holding it as if it were a grasshopper. Her hand shakes slightly as she turns her wrist, lifts the doughnut to her mouth, takes a small bite, and chews. After a little while, effortfully, she swallows.

"Quite nice," she says, her eyes watering.

I pick another piece for myself off the plate. "Just as well this is the last one. I could pig out on these."

"You're lucky," says Isabel. "You can eat what you want."

We drink our tea, and in spite of everything we're more relaxed together than we've been for a long time. Isabel doesn't light any more cigarettes. Her piece of doughnut lies on the plate, the cream melting into a yellow puddle. The cuffs of her soft red shirt lie loosely on her slender wrists. She turns a ring on the little finger of her right hand, a turquoise and silver ring she bought in Kashmir, long before she met Richard. She brought me back a bracelet, made of the same turquoise, with silver links that turned black when I wore it.

"But there's the baby," says Isabel abruptly, out of some long, private train of thought.

"That might make things better."

"The trouble is, men need sex."

It's such an odd thing to say, so unlike Isabel, but at the same time so truly Isabelline that I smile. Isabel flushes slightly.

"They do," I say.

"I don't, though, do you? Not really. You soon get used to not having it. I remember thinking the same about food. All those people thinking they had to have food all the time or they'd die, always thinking about it and talking about it and going out to the shops for it and then sitting chomping it down, and yet it wasn't really necessary at all. All the world turned on something you could do without. I wanted to shout out and tell everyone the truth."

"But you didn't."

"Oh no," says Isabel. "That sort of thing you keep to yourself, don't you?" She smiles, a real, curling smile, as if we're conspirators. I remember her telling me Sunday school was shit and freeing me forever from wanting to bow down to anything.

"You don't need to worry about Richard," I say. "There are plenty of other people in the world who like sex."

"That's what I keep hoping."

"Don't worry about it. He'll be fine."

One word more would be too many. We hover on the edge of what can't be said, caught up, as we used to be caught in the histories we made up for Rosina and Mandy. They were always changing. That was the best thing about the dolls. If the storyline didn't work out, we could wipe out their pasts. Suddenly I remember how Isabel decided one summer that Rosina had long raven hair.

"What's raven?"

"Black."

"But Rosina's got yellow hair."

"That doesn't matter. It's raven now," said Isabel, picking up the dolls' hairbrush.

"Is it?"

"Of course it is. It's part of the game. Now you say, *Are you going to brush Rosina's raven hair?*"

"Are you going to brush Rosina's raven hair, Isabel?" I asked. I squinted at the doll. On her coarse, vigorous, yellow hair I thought I detected a faint sheen of black.

*   *   *

"As long as Richard's happy, I don't mind," says Isabel.

"You want to stay together."

"Yes, why not?"

"There's no reason why not."

I go downstairs with the empty mugs and pot rattling on the tray. It's half-past five. The zone of safety is nearly over: the earliest train Edward could catch comes in at five-fifteen. But even if he gets that train, he'll have to ring for a taxi at the station, and that'll take a while to come. And then there's Susan, walking back over the fields from the farm. She shouldn't be back for a while yet.

Richard is slicing tomatoes into a bowl.

"You haven't skinned them."

"It's not worth it."

"It's those little touches that make all the difference."

"I'm sure." He puts down the knife. "You were a long time."

"We were just talking."

"Do you want to go in the garden?"

"No." Isabel's hand is on me. Her permission freezes me. "No, I'm not —"

"I see." He goes on slicing tomatoes, expertly, his face closed.

"You don't. You don't see anything." I take the knife

out of his hand. Not the garden, because the garden is Isabel's place. But the kitchen, here, with juice dripping off the knife and cream souring, that's my place. The door to the passage is half-open, and the back door too. But there's nothing anywhere but the dead quiet of late afternoon. I pull my T-shirt over my head.

"What are you doing?"

"You can see what I'm doing."

"Jesus, Nina. Isabel might come down any minute."

"She won't."

"And we can't lie on this floor. Look at the muck down there."

"We'll do it standing up against the stove."

"Is it off?"

"Of course it's off."

We lean together. There's no time to spare, but I'm weak with slowness. I want to do everything as if it's for the first time. Unbutton each button, slide it out of its little sewn nest. Pull back his shirt. Lie against his chest, sinking into the thickness of his flesh with my heart thudding as if I'm still running over the fields. I shut my eyes.

He shoves me upright. "Nina, get your clothes on. There's a car."

I stoop, grab my T-shirt off the floor, pull it over my head, stand up again, dizzy. The car engine's stopped, and there are voices.

"Edward."

We move apart. Richard sits down at the table and picks up the knife. I turn the cold tap full on in a noisy gush and put a saucepan underneath it. Water bounces up from the bare metal and spatters me. The car engine starts again and footsteps crunch, stop, crunch on again, past the kitchen door.

"He's going in through the garden."

We look at each other, and I push back my hair with a wet hand.

"He's going to stay here till I go back to London. He won't leave us alone," I say.

"Do you think he's guessed?"

"He knows."

"Does he." Richard's face is tense, focused. This is what he must look like at work, an economist working out the odds on growth in a small, unstable economy.

"But he won't say anything," I say. "This suits him, really. He's got Isabel to himself. Hours of talk in the bedroom while we're out of the way."

"You can't be sure of that. He'll do anything for her."

The levels of what I'm capable of buzz and shift in my head. "I'm going to go back to London tomorrow," I say, as if it's long planned. I watch for the tiny shrinkage of his pupils in his still face, the sign of disappointment he can't hide.

chapter *twenty*

"I WANT US to have a celebration," says Isabel. We all turn: Richard from the paper, Edward from the floor, where he's assembling the mobile he's bought for the baby in London. I look up from spreading toast with black cherry jam.

It's too hot already, and riding toward the 93 degrees forecast for today, although it's only half-past eight. All the windows are open. It was too hot to sleep, and the baby howled from two until four. I kept listening for rain, the way I used to listen for the sea. The ground's as hard and tight as a drum. All night I slid in and out of sleep, and I woke up aching. It's oppressively close this morning.

"A celebration?"

"Yes. I couldn't sleep because it was so hot, and I've been thinking about it all night. We ought to do something, before you all go. We're never going to get a summer like this again, with all of you staying here. And Susan's leaving soon, so I thought we'd ask her and

Margery as well. But not anyone else, no one from London. Just us."

The line between Isabel's eyes has become a deep groove. She glances round at us all, her eyes very bright. If I touched Isabel now she'd spark.

"Don't you think it's a good idea?"

"What sort of celebration?" asks Richard.

I know what he means, but Isabel answers a different question. "A dinner. We'll eat outside, on the terrace. We'll take the long table out, and hang those candle-lanterns in the apple trees for when it gets dark. There's that white cloth your mother gave us, Richard, the linen one with the ivy pattern. And the triple candlestick. Candles will burn outside as well as they do indoors in this weather."

"It'll be a lot of work for Nina," says Richard, looking at me. "That salmon took you most of the day, didn't it?"

"It won't be left to her," says Isabel sharply. "We'll all do it together. We'll each choose a dish, and cook it."

"A family feast," says Edward. It's impossible to tell if his tone is pleased or ironic. Against my will, I start to warm to the idea, and see what it could be like. The table loaded, the cloth crowded with bottles and flowers, the blue dusk, and then the candles. A feast to end everything that's happened here and set us free from one another. A feast that'll put a shape round our confusion and give it a name. But I was going to go home today, and it's so hot. My skin itches at the thought of all that shopping, and the car cooking in its own fumes on roads full of people desperate to get to the sea.

Richard goes over to the window. "It looks like thunder," he remarks, as if this has nothing to do with Isabel's plan.

"It won't rain. It's been like this for weeks," says Isabel quickly.

"Look at those clouds over there."

It looks as if someone has drawn shapes on the sky with a metallic pen. They're the faintest of outlines, gathering in the distance.

"That's nothing," says Edward. "It won't rain, the forecast said it'd be even hotter this afternoon. It's going to beat all the records. Do you know this is the hottest summer there's been for two hundred years?"

"We need rain," says Richard.

"How would you know? You spend half your life up in the air," says Isabel.

"You can see a lot from a plane."

"So, when's this celebration going to be?" asks Edward.

"I thought we'd have it tonight. There's plenty of time, if we each work out what we're going to cook now, and then you and Richard and Nina go and do all the shopping. You'll have to go into Brighton to get everything. If you and Richard carry the table and chairs out first, then Susan can decorate them while you're out. I want flowers everywhere, and ivy, and vine leaves. I'll look after the baby."

"Are you sure you're up to this, Isabel? You know how tired you are," says Richard.

But Isabel is flushed, electric. "Of course I'm all right. At least I'll be doing something, instead of sitting around waiting for the baby to cry."

"It's a fantastic idea," says Edward, getting up. He's put together the frame of the mobile, and now he reaches up to hang it from a hook on the back of the door. "You'll have to put a hook in the ceiling for this, Isabel, over the baby's bed." There are dozens of blue wooden fish in the box. One by one Edward takes them out and threads them into place. The mobile is going to be a huge cage of fish.

"How many fish are there?" asks Richard.

"Forty."

"It'll take up half the room. He won't be able to see the sky."

"It's beautiful," says Isabel.

"He'll grow up believing that fish can fly," I say.

"Does that matter?"

"Of course it matters. What kind of a picture of the world is he going to have?"

"A better one than we had," says Isabel. Her fingers

play with the light, dry fish. The fish we saw flopping in the bottom of fishing boats in our childhood weren't like that. They had weight, and muscle. They were slippery when you picked them up, their blood was bright, like human blood, and their eyes looked as if they were watching you. On a good day you could get a shopping bag full of herring for a shilling. We ate a lot of herring.

The mobile is a tangle of wood and thread, but Edward works his way through it confidently. We're all watching him now, the way people watch anyone who's doing something with his hands. Isabel picks up another fish. "There," says Edward, pointing, "slip the thread through the little hook." The thread is plastic, and invisible from where I am, but Isabel ties nothing to nothing, and there the fish hangs.

"That's going to take you forever," says Susan, coming in with Antony asleep at last, his face puffed and blotched.

"It won't take long."

Isabel and Edward work together, and I wonder if I'm the only one who sees how alike they are. I watch their slender fingers, their fine, concentrated faces. They could be brother and sister. They are so much more alike than Isabel and me. Next to them I look like a peasant, and so does Richard. Richard's watching them too, as they construct the mobile for his son.

"We'll get this finished," says Edward, "and then

we'll plan tonight. We'll have to have music. Are you well enough to dance?"

"If it's a slow number," says Isabel.

"What's happening tonight?" asks Susan.

"There's going to be a party," says Richard, his voice and face expressionless.

"Not a party, a celebration," says Isabel, her mouth full of thread.

"What's the difference?"

"A party's open to anyone. This is private."

"I'll go home for the evening, then," says Susan stiffly.

"Oh no, Susan, I didn't mean that. You've got to come. You must come. Please. It won't be the same without you."

Isabel stretches out her hand to Susan, pleading, and Susan melts at once. She'll come, of course she will, and so will her mother. All we have to think about now is what we're going to cook.

"Six courses," says Isabel.

"But you can't just have six of anything. You have to plan it so the dishes work together." It's so obvious it shouldn't need to be said.

"They're separate courses anyway, so it doesn't matter," says Isabel, turning her obstinate, beautiful face toward me without really looking at me. I can't put into words how a meal should be, how there should be pauses, and tiny repetitions, reactions of taste against taste. How it should build from the first note, then die down again. Isabel won't think about any of that. She won't consider the colors and textures of food, because she doesn't want to give it that much attention. Food has been crushed down into a small space in Isabel's mind. Six courses: one for each of us except Antony. Why should anyone count Antony? But if there's going to be a celebration I can't think of anything apart from his existence that we can possibly be celebrating. I could make a cake and ice his name on it.

No one's asked why Isabel wants a feast, when she won't eat anything at it. This house is stiff with things that can't be said. What we say sounds more like code than conversation. But who wrote the code? Who's forcing us to use it?

"When are you leaving, Nina?" asks Richard in front of everyone.

"I was thinking of going today, but I'll wait till tomorrow now."

"I'll miss you, Neen," says Isabel, with a quick, public smile. "It's been lovely having you here for so long."

She's very tense. She pulls a plastic thread too hard and it snaps, but Edward ties it up in an invisible knot and it's all right. Isabel sits back on her heels, blinking and wiping her hands, which are wet with sweat. "I can't do it, Edward," she says in a voice blank with distress. Then, visibly, she gathers herself together. "It's hurting my eyes. Nina, have you thought of what you're going to do for the meal yet?"

I haven't thought at all, but I don't need to. "Figs," I say.

"Figs?"

"Yes. Black Turkish figs. They're just coming into season. I saw some the other day. A huge plate of fresh figs so we can have as many as we want for once. We could eat them at the beginning of the meal, or at the end. They won't spoil the taste of whatever comes next. I'll whip some cream to go with them, though I think they're better without."

"You're not going to cook, then?"

"Isabel, they'll be perfect, I promise you. Better than anything I could cook. I'll probably make something else as well, but that's a surprise."

"Oh!" She relaxes. "You *are* cooking something, then."

The figs mean nothing to her. Their white paper packing, the fragile, bloomy skin of each fruit, the way the seeds ooze slowly through cracks in the flesh, the fleshy fatness at the base of the stem. I bought figs in Dubrovnik market once, before it was shelled. The market women laid them out on leaves, and when you looked closely you could see tiny fissures, like a crazy paving of sweetness, because the fruit was ripe to burst-

ing. I ate figs and oranges with black coffee every morning, and I found out that figs are never one color. They're
black, then purple, but they always have some green left
in them too, and as the skin grows thinner you see the
brown-gold of flesh through it.

I see Richard swallow.

"What about all of you?"

"I'll make a fish soup," Edward says. "If we're going
into Brighton I know a good fishmonger there. Shrimp
and garlic soup with coriander. It's the fish stock that
takes the time."

Fish stock is easy, as we both know, but Edward is
scoring points this morning. "Or there's a Galician fish
stew I've been wanting to try out," he muses. "But you
have to boil up olive oil and water to cook the fish, and
the timing's tricky — if the emulsion's not right the fish
boils to rags —"

"Make the soup."

"I know what I can bring," says Susan. "My mum's
got an ice-cream maker, and she's made boxes and boxes
for the Young Farmers — it's all in the freezer. There's
gooseberry crumble ice cream, and butterscotch, and
raspberry. I'll put one of each in a freezer pack and
bring it over."

"I thought I'd make a fruit salad," says Isabel.

Now there's a tradition of my mother's that Isabel has
kept up. A sodden mass of tinned peaches and cocktail

cherries in colorless syrup, brought to life by a quarter-pound of green grapes and a couple of oranges hacked into slices. If my mother was feeling reckless she would tip in a glass of brandy to add smolder to the tang of metal and sugar. Always cheap brandy. She could never really stop being careful. But Isabel isn't doing the shopping, and I think I can remember a recipe for mango and peach slices with fresh lime and ginger syrup.

"Do you mind what fruit we get, or shall we just buy whatever looks good?"

"Oh, anything," says Isabel. "I've got loads of tins. I think I've even got a tin of litchis somewhere."

"That seems to leave me with the main course," says Richard.

"I know what you can do. It'll fit in with everything perfectly, and it isn't difficult," I say. "Roasted vegetables with couscous in layers with goat cheese. We'll do aubergines and red peppers and courgettes and little onions. It sounds a mess but it's good. You could do tabbouleh as a side dish, and goat cheese in filo pastry parcels."

"Christ, Nina."

Isabel laughs. "There you are, Richard."

"Okay. This is what you've got to do. Don't cook the couscous, let it soak for ten minutes in boiling stock. That works better. There's stock in the fridge, and you can chop a couple of leaves of mint into it after you've boiled it up, then strain it again. You only want an edge of mint in the couscous. The peppers need to be seared. If they're sweet enough you'll get that black, sticky taste from the skin, almost a toffee taste. And that'll bring out the sweetness in the onions too. All the other stuff's easy: we'll buy the filo pastry from the Greek shop and the cheese too. It's always fresh there. And those fat squashy olives."

"Easy," says Richard.

"It's okay, I'll help you. Let me just write down olive oil. That stuff I bought in the village is no good. And bread." I write on the back of an envelope. "Cheese. Champagne. How many bottles? I'm paying."

"No, you're not," says Richard quickly. "You're not paying for anything this time, Nina."

"So put your purse away," says Isabel.

We smile. We smile like sisters, like what we should be instead of what we are. For a second Edward's the family friend who's splurged on an expensive toy for the baby to whom he'll be unofficial uncle. Richard is the proud father going out to buy champagne to wet the head of his first son. Isabel is the young mother who's had a bad time but is getting back on her feet now. And I'm the aunt, the sister-in-law, the sister, the friend. The cook. Whatever you want.

"There," says Edward. "That's done." Carefully, he

unhooks the finished mobile from the back of the door. He holds the frame where the two pieces of wood cross, and gives it a small shake. The fish shiver into position. The wires bounce a little, the threads go up and down, the fish wince then start to swim through the air. Isabel claps her hands.

"It's wonderful, Edward. I never thought it would be so beautiful." There's too much emotion in her voice again, as there was when she pleaded with Susan, but Edward doesn't seem to notice. He smiles as he pushes the mobile again with one finger and all the fish turn. There's a tiny clacking sound as their wooden fins touch. Edward's face is proud and absorbed.

"Antony's going to love this," he says, as if Antony's a person with tastes of his own.

"So we're going into town," says Richard, standing up. "We'd better finish that list."

"It doesn't need all three of us to go. I'll stay with you, Isabel," says Edward.

But Isabel leans back in her chair and shuts her eyes. "You go. You need to get all the stuff for your fish soup."

"I can write it all down for them, and stay with you. You don't want to be on your own."

"I shan't be on my own, I've got Susan. Really, Edward, I'd much rather you went. You've been stuck in with me since you got here. You could all have lunch out together, and I'll sleep for a couple of hours or I'll be dead later on. Susan'll do the table, then she can mind Antony, can't you, Susan?"

"If you're tired, the baby can always come out with me while I do the table as well. He's no trouble. And I'll ring Mum, shall I, about tonight?"

"I'll ring her," says Isabel.

"We'll get that table moved then, Edward," says Richard. Even the way he says it sounds grim and masculine. They get up, facing each other, two men who don't like each other but are used to having to get along. Now that they're face to face I realize just how much dislike there is. Their bodies know it. They move into position like boxers, and there are patches of sweat under Richard's arms already, before they've even started lifting. They go out together.

"What flowers shall I pick?" asks Susan.

"Whatever you like," says Isabel. "Pick everything." She says it carelessly and Susan nods, because she has no way of knowing that this is something Isabel could never possibly mean. She doesn't like picking any flowers for the house at all, though she gives way grudgingly and puts a few roses on the table when people are coming. Isabel would know if two heads of white phlox were cut from her border. She knows which rose is ready to drop its petals at a touch.

"Cut the black dahlias. And the Japanese anemones

have come out early because of the heat. They'd look good with the dahlias," she tells Susan. The black dahlias are rare. I've never seen their tiny velvet flowers in any other garden. They have bronze leaves, and Isabel has planted them in a mass in front of a sage bush. They are never cut for the house.

"Where are those, then?" asks Susan.

"Go down past the cherry tree, they're in the bed on your left, by the wall. No, never mind, I'll cut them for you. But take anything else you want from the garden, Susan. Cut what you like," repeats Isabel, her veiled, cloudy eyes turned in my direction. Her hand dangles by the spread quilt where Susan has laid the baby. She does not quite touch him, but an inch closer and her fingers would brush his lips.